THE
ANDREAN
PROJECT

First published 2016 by DB Publishing, an imprint of JMD Media Ltd, Nottingham, United Kingdom.

ISBN 9781780915333

THE
ANDREAN
PROJECT

IAN C. SIMPSON

In memory of David F. Simpson WS
1919–1994

'The British Amateur
– The Most Important Tournament of My Life'
Bobby Jones, Golf is My Game

AUTHOR'S NOTE

As with *Sons of the Fathers* I have tried to weave a wholly fictitious murder mystery into an authentic account of a highly significant golf tournament. Almost all the people I have brought
into the story are creatures of my imagination except the Jones
party and the first six competitors, Jones' actual opponents,
named in the list of characters at the start of the book. Any
resemblance the rest may have to persons living or dead is
coincidental.

I said almost. Jimmy Alexander was the Old Course starter
for some decades. A.B. Paterson was a stalwart of St Andrews
theatricals for many years, notable for his work in the famous
Byre Theatre, which he founded in 1933. Norman Boase is also
mentioned. He was in fact the provost of St Andrews in 1930.
As Hector remarks, he would never have allowed the situation
I describe to come about. It was necessary for the purposes
of the plot to terminate his period of office early and promote
an inadequate, and fictitious, replacement. Lastly, MacGregor
Mitchell KC was the unofficial leader of the Scottish criminal
bar at the time. He was also my great-uncle; I was privileged to
wear his horsehair wig throughout my own professional career.
I hope my literary nepotism will be forgiven.

When writing about real people I have tried to have them
act in character. In the case of Jones I have used quotes from
my sources. His victory speech was quoted verbatim in the
next weekday's newspaper. I have taken some liberty with O.B.
Keeler and Sidney Roper. The latter, an unsung competitor who
came close to making Jones fall at the first fence in his epic
endeavour, seemed to make a promising man of mystery. About

the former, Jones wrote: 'Whatever the mood, Keeler was the ideal companion. He had read almost everything and remembered most of it; he could, and frequently did, recite verse for hours ... he was an acutely sensitive, instinctively gallant and wholly unselfish friend whose loyalty and devotion could never once be questioned.' It was not fanciful of me to ascribe to him an intimate knowledge of *Macbeth*.

I have relied on archive material from *The Scotsman*; also *Golf is my Game*, Bobby Jones; *The Bobby Jones Story,* O.B. Keeler; *St Andrews, Home of Golf* and *About St Andrews – and About*, both by James K. Robertson.

Thanks go to Steve Caron and all at DB Publishing. With any factual errors, the buck stops with me.

Ian C. Simpson

List of characters you will meet and those associated with them:

The Drummond household:
Sheriff Hector Drummond
Lavender Drummond, his wife
Jake Drummond, his stepson
Marie and Charlotte Drummond, his daughters
Mrs Alves, their housekeeper

The Jones party:
Bobby Jones
Mary Jones, his wife
O.B. Keeler, his biographer
Eleanor Keeler, O.B.'s wife
Jack McIntyre, Jones' caddie

St Andrews caddies:
Tommy Addison
Jeannie Addison, his sister
'Stuartie'

The police:
Inspector McTaggart, Cupar
Sergeant McNeill, St Andrews
PC Graham Gemmell, St Andrews

The courts:
Sheriff Principal Crichton 'Fatty' Fairweather, KC, Hector's superior
Forbes, Hector's bar officer
Newton, the local procurator fiscal, who prosecutes
Hotchkiss, a local solicitor
MacGregor Mitchell, KC, an eminent senior counsel

Competitors in the Amateur Championship:
Sidney Roper, Nottingham
Cyril Tolley, England
Harrison 'Jimmie' Johnston, USA
Eric Fiddian, England
George Voigt, New York
Roger Wethered, England
Laurence Fishburne, St Andrews
Brian Maxwell, USA

St Andrews citizens:
Gordon Macmillan, a solicitor
Lucy Macmillan, his wife
Sorley Macmillan, their son
Alex B. Paterson, director of *Macbeth*
Alan Corbett
Jane Corbett, his wife
Dr Doris Moncur
Willie Moncur, her brother, a golf professional
'Bean' Hamilton
Freddie Torkington
Fiona Torkington, his wife
Daisy, the Torkington's maid
Jim Liddell
Mary, telephone operator/receptionist at the Grand Hotel
Courtney Haversham, MP
Bert Wilson, his valet
Dan Saunderson, a fishmonger

Others:
Dr Henry Fallon, Perth
Janet Fallon, his wife
Bailey, head porter at Gleneagles
Other people of little importance to the narrative are named
in the text.

SCOTLAND
EARLY MAY 1930

1

'Not bad. Where did you get it?' Sorley Macmillan smacked his lips and inspected the label of the sherry bottle.

Jake Drummond lounged on the narrow, lumpy bed in his friend's basically furnished study. 'Guess.'

'Smuggled from home?'

'Cold.'

'You bribed a groundsman?'

'Still cold.'

Sorley looked out of the window. While the long shadows of an early May evening covered most of Glenalmond's Front Quad, sunshine brought out the red in the sandstone wall opposite. The prestigious boys' boarding school nestling in the Perthshire hills was looking its best. 'You didn't pinch it, did you?' His voice betrayed a tremor of fear.

Jake smiled like a Cheshire cat. He reached over for the bottle and swallowed until he choked. He wiped his mouth with the back of his hand. 'What if I did?' He handed the bottle back.

'Brave thing to do.' Sorley let the glass touch his lips.

'You're just sipping.'

Sorley looked his friend in the eye and drank deeply. 'Where did you take it from?'

Jake wondered about keeping him guessing. He took

another swig and saw the bottle was half empty. 'The masters' common room,' he whispered.

'How? When?'

'A couple of days ago. I was late for lunch so didn't show up at all. The common room door was open and the cupboard was unlocked. Easy-peasy.'

'Strange they didn't notice.'

'This bottle was at the back. There was a nearly-full one open.'

'Right.' Sorley took another sip, his waning enthusiasm obvious. 'Aren't you going to keep some?'

'I've promised myself I'd get squiffy tonight.'

'Why?'

'Fifteen years ago today,' he paused, 'my real father was killed at Ypres.' Tears pricking his eyes, Jake got off the bed and breathed deeply at the open window.

'I didn't think about ...'

'Few do. To hell. Drink up.'

Sorley obeyed and Jake sat back down. They passed the bottle to and fro in morose silence.

'Second best,' Jake muttered after a while.

'What do you mean?'

'Papa – Uncle Hector, when I was small. Only he's not my papa. He's not even a real uncle. He was second best for my mother, and he's second best for me.'

'I like the Sheriff.'

'Oh, he's a good chap. But blood's thicker than water. He's said that to me himself. He doesn't really think of me as his son, though he pretends.' He shook his head.

'Everyone here pretends,' Jake continued. 'We all troop into chapel but half of us don't believe a word of the hogwash they preach. They go on about duty and moral fibre, but that's just so we'll be good, brave little fellows and die cheerfully for our country the next time some statesman decides to have a war. "The first hundred thousand will represent the College, sorry, the country against Germany in France ..."'

'It's not as bad as that ...'

'As if it were a bloody rugger match ...'

'No need to get bolshie ...'

'Yes there bloody is. What did a sense of duty do for my real father? It got him a bullet, that's what.'

'But we won the War. Because of men like him.'

'He may be a hero, but he's dead. Away. Up there, in the sky. Or deep in the mud. He got to see me toddling, that's all. And I can't remember him.' He paused for another swallow. There was not much left in the bottle. 'I saw Earl Haig once, years ago,' he said, his voice quiet. 'Strutting into the R and A as if he owned it. Papa called him "The man who won the war". Callous, murdering bastard, more like.'

Sorley spread his hands in front of him. 'It's terrible luck for you, but ...'

'We've just got to take whatever comes our way. If you really believe that, bugger you, Sorley. Bugger everyone here.' He jumped up then hurled the bottle through the open window. He watched as the brown glass somersaulted down and shattered on the paved surface of the quad, close to where two masters were taking an evening stroll. Startled, they both jumped then looked up.

'They'll see it's my window, you bloody fool.' Sorley tugged Jake back.

'I'll take the blame,' Jake said, steadying himself on the sill. 'We St Andrews boys must stand up for each other. I suppose you'd better not be here when they find me.'

Sorley stood indecisively, looking at his friend. 'What have you done, Jake?' he said. He made for the door, checked the corridor was clear, then stepped out, turning the handle slowly and quietly behind him. Trying to look natural, he walked towards the washrooms at the end, his footsteps loud on the polished wooden floor.

'Macmillan! Where do you think you're going?' Sorley turned to see Harrigan, the Classics master, at the other end of the corridor. He was breathing heavily as he advanced, his index finger pointing accusingly.

2

Three weeks later

'Lady Macbeth? Wow, that's a challenging role.' Bobby Jones smiled admiringly at Lavender Drummond, his hostess. 'And your first night is Tuesday?'

'You'll have to put on your meanest face. Save the milk of human kindness for home.' O.B. Keeler, the owlish American who chronicled Bobby Jones' achievements, sipped his claret then brought a forkful of roast beef and Yorkshire pudding to his mouth.

'Some milk of human kindness would be nice here,' Jake Drummond said. '*Macbeth* is one of the books I have to know for my exams, so I help Mama with her words, shift scenery and play odd parts. She keeps me hard at it.' His confident manner belied the fact that three weeks earlier he and his best friend, Sorley Macmillan, had been summarily expelled from Glenalmond.

'It'll be worth it. Culture apart, it's a great feeling when you hear you've passed an exam, and the older you are, the bigger the feeling of relief,' Jones told him in his honey-smooth Georgia drawl. 'Do you hope to go to university here in St Andrews? I've seen a lot of students in their red gowns. They look mighty fine.'

'I'm trying for Oxford, but if they won't have me it'll be
Edinburgh. If they'll take me,' he added quickly. 'It's better to
get away from home. For a bit.'

'Sow your wild oats somewhere else?' O.B. said, eyes twin-
kling behind round glasses.

Sheriff Hector Drummond cleared his throat and went to
carve more beef from the joint. Sunday lunch was his favourite meal and Bobby Jones, Bob to friends and family, was his
sporting hero. He had got to know him and O.B. when they
had helped him solve a series of murders at the time of the
1927 Open. Defying his absurdly pompous superior, Sheriff
Principal Crichton 'Fatty' Fairweather KC, he had taken on
an investigative role that was no part of his duties as the local
judge, and they had provided invaluable help. Three years on,
he felt greatly honoured that they, with their wives, should
come for lunch the day before the British Amateur Championship got under way. He could scarcely believe that the stocky,
fair-haired young man, a warm and gracious guest with a ready
smile, was the grim-faced competitor with an iron determination to win if he fairly could that the rest of the world knew
and admired.

The mahogany dining table, adorned with silver and crystal, looked splendid and Mrs Alves, their housekeeper/nanny,
had excelled in the kitchen. Hector had asked Tommy Addison, the caddie who had risked his life helping him in 1927, to
help serve. He too practically worshipped Jones. Making up the
party was Hector's stepson, Jake. Hector wished he were back
at school, where he should be. An Old Glenalmond himself, he
had not forgiven him for the humiliation of being summoned by
a telephone call from the Warden: 'Please collect your son as
soon as possible. He has let you down very badly.'

'Is Hector in the play? From the way he wields that carving

knife, I can tell he'd make a great murderer,' O.B. said with a puckish grin.

'Papa's too nice to stick the knife right in, even if Mama told him to,' Jake said, his face flushed with claret. 'I'm a murderer, actually. Macduff's son calls me a "shag-haired villain" …'

'Good casting. Under that slimy Brylcreem muck, your hair's far too long,' Hector interjected.

Undeterred, Jake got to his feet. 'I say: "What! You egg. Young fry of treachery!" Then I stab him.' With gusto, he thrust his knife into an imaginary victim. 'It's fun, but I have to be careful I don't really stab him – or giggle.'

'It sure doesn't sound much like any Shakespeare I've heard.' Mary Jones grinned, her dark eyes sparkling.

'Perhaps Jake has found a new edition,' Bob said.

O.B. clapped his hands and said 'Bravo' as the young actor sat down.

His carving knife dripping gravy, Hector turned from the joint. 'You can see we have more than enough thespians in the family. I just hope I'll wield my putter with deadly effect this week.'

'Well, I'm glad I haven't been drawn against your husband,' Bob said.

'Why?' Lavender failed to keep the surprise out of her voice. The British Amateur was the first of the year's four major golf championships, and it was well known that Jones' preparations for 'The 1930 Campaign' had surpassed what he had done in any previous year. That week, as usual, he was the clear favourite to win. By contrast, Hector had entered simply because he had got his handicap low enough to do so. His modest objectives were to win a game then avoid ignominious defeat in the second round.

Bob grinned. 'In 1921 at Hoylake, there was a little man

called Hamlet, who played in one of those high, starched collars and a bow tie. He nearly beat me ...'

'He scored some "very palpable hits" on Bob,' O.B. interrupted.

'I played badly. The experience left me apprehensive about opponents who remind me of Shakespeare's tragedies, such as Lady Macbeth's husband.'

'Don't they call *Macbeth* "The Scotch play" for some reason?' Eleanor Keeler asked.

'Theatrical types say it's unlucky,' Hector said. 'Baloney, of course. It's just that there are a lot of murders in it. I believe some actor chap got himself killed by accident. Slip of the knife, or something. Anyway, Bob, you should be safe enough tomorrow. Shakespeare never got round to writing *Sidney Roper*. From what I hear, he's a level fives man.'

Bob winced. 'I don't want to hear that. It's possible for any competitor in this championship to beat me over eighteen holes. Everyone playing is capable of scoring under eighty, on his day. And if I play badly I can be over eighty. When I meet Mr Sidney Roper tomorrow afternoon I shall give him my full attention and respect.'

'I gather from *The Scotsman* you had an interesting practice game with Miss Wethered on Friday,' Lavender said.

'Joyce is a terrific player,' Bob said. 'If she hadn't fallen away at the end she'd have beaten all three of us.'

'She's better than most of your Walker Cup team,' O.B. said. 'I've even heard British gentlemen opine that she could play number three or four, if only they'd let the ladies in.'

'Pity she's not playing in the Amateur, so she could beat a man,' Jake said, glancing at Hector.

No-one rose to this remark. Outside, pink rhododendrons and brilliant yellow laburnums swayed in the cool east wind.

Tommy Addison came in to clear the plates and the diners muttered their appreciation of the meal.

'That was your fault!' Jake spat out, as Tommy tipped gravy over O.B.'s sleeve.

'Sorry, sir, sorry.' Tommy blushed and, in his confusion, nearly dropped the plate he had balanced on his forearm.

'Don't worry, son. I'll go sponge it now, and it'll never show.' O.B. got up. 'I've spilled drinks on most of my best friends. Right, Bob?'

'They've certainly spilled plenty on you,' Eleanor Keeler commented dryly.

'I think you'll find, Jake, that it's unwise to stretch suddenly for your wine glass while waiters are trying to do their job.' Bob's tone was light, but his steady gaze across the table made Jake look down.

'Isn't it time you started your afternoon's revision?' Hector asked Jake, who made no move.

'We haven't had pudding yet, darling,' Lavender said firmly. 'It's clootie dumpling, and Mrs Alves tells me she gave it an extra skelp as she put it in the pot to boil. It's for luck,' she added, miming a smack for the Americans' benefit.

'It's not the only thing round here that could do with an extra skelp,' Hector muttered, glancing at Jake.

'I can't wait to try it,' Mary said, although her tone was doubtful. 'Eleanor's told me about it many times.'

There was no mistaking the beam on Eleanor's face when Mrs Alves carried in her *piece de resistance*.

Inwardly seething, Hector poured more claret for everyone except Jake as a red-faced Tommy brought in the pudding plates.

'This is undoing all the good work I did over the winter,' Bob said, digging his spoon into the rich, dense dumpling. He began to describe the game, played with a light tennis racket

and a heavy shuttlecock, invented by his friend Douglas Fairbanks, which he had played during recent months.

After lunch, on Lavender's command, Jake went upstairs
to study. In the drawing room, Hector produced a decanter of
port, Warre's 1904. He had another bottle in the pantry, but it
was not required. After a relaxed afternoon and a walk round
the garden, Hector drove his guests back to the Grand Hotel,
the distinctive red sandstone building behind the eighteenth
green of the Old Course, O.B. swearing that the woods at the
nearby Balgove Farm were moving inexorably towards them.

*   *   *

'You'll get some distinguished people in your audience on Tuesday,' Hector said to Lavender when he returned. 'It's a pity
Douglas Fairbanks hasn't stayed on after the Walker Cup to see
Bob play in the Amateur. He might have offered you a role in
one of his films.'

'That would put the St Andrews Amateur Dramatic Society
on the map. Imagine Hollywood movie men queuing up outside
the church hall to watch us! Americans certainly do things in
style; "Doug" crossed the Atlantic just to see his friend play
golf,' Lavender said.

'One thing, old girl.' Hector cleared his throat then paused.
'I really think Jake behaved badly when he made Tommy spill
over O.B.'

Lavender replied sharply, 'It was an accident, Hector, and
Tommy was clumsy.'

Hector raised an eyebrow. 'He's gone very funny recently.
Jake, I mean. I don't know quite how to handle him. I just can't
get over him getting expelled when Glenalmond seemed to suit
him so well.'

'I've said this before, but I think that Macmillan boy led him on.'

'Jake still says he didn't.'

'Well, I'm glad they were expelled together. When Jake tried to take all the blame, the Warden saw that he was being noble. It's a pity if you can't.'

Hector did not want to spoil a famous day, but there was something else troubling him. The subject had become increasingly awkward for both of them as the years had passed, but alcohol had loosened his tongue. He took a cigarette from his case and tapped the loose tobacco out with unnecessary vehemence before flicking his scuffed lighter. It had belonged to Jake's father, his best friend.

'The day he got drunk, old girl, it was fifteen years exactly since John …'

'I know.'

'Do you think …?'

'I don't know what to think.'

'I feel I'm his father yet not his father, don't you know? More so recently.'

'Bear with him, Hector, please. I think he's mixed-up, surely you can understand that?'

'I suppose I do, but it was he who wanted to change his surname to Drummond, just three years ago.'

'We must carry on as normal, darling. He's young, remember. And please try not to get cross with him. It doesn't help.'

'I do try, but, well, he should be more ashamed of himself, and he's so damned disrespectful …'

'Mama, Papa, look!' Marie and Charlotte, nine and seven respectively and deemed too young to join the lunch party, burst into the room waving newly created works of art. Both Hector and Lavender were grateful for the diversion.

3

In the quietness of dawn, the buck rabbit hopped about the grassy clearing in the whin bushes. Droplets of water hung in the air and settled equally on the abundant yellow blossom and the cruel, protective needles. It was cold for early summer but the new growth tasted sweet and good. At one point the rabbit's nose twitched. There was an odd, cloying taste to the fresh, green grass. He moved on and found sticky stuff was clinging to his fur. Something big lay nearby. He sat up, looked round, licked his paws and went to feed elsewhere. He didn't care, but he had just encountered vintage port, human blood and a body.

4

As the swirling North Sea *haar* cleared from the Old Course, Hector shook hands with his first-round opponent. Another member of the Royal and Ancient who had entered without prospect of significant success, Laurence Fishburne was someone Hector knew he could beat. This was the moment he had been anticipating for months. He had spent hours hitting practice balls on the New Course, copying Jones' narrow stance and little forward twist of the hips before taking the club back. Now he was striking the ball as well as he had ever done. But it was one thing to do it in practice. This was the real thing. A twitchy smile told Hector that Fishburne was as nervous as he was.

The *haar* had delayed the start of play, keeping them hanging about for a stomach-churning half hour. 'Keep yer energy fur the match, sir,' Tommy had said, interrupting Hector's frantic practice swings, and returning the driver to the bag. Instead, Hector marched up and down the closely-mown teeing ground, blowing on his hands and swinging his arms. Although locals expected warm sunshine by mid-morning, damp air chilled the early starters to the bone. Hector shivered under a fashionable but thin turtleneck sweater and regretted not wearing the shapeless, woolly pullover that had seen many winters. He glanced at the Big Window of the Royal and Ancient, half-wishing he was among the sages gathered there, warm and comfortable in their leather arm chairs, commenting on the first tee swings of the competitors.

The match ahead had passed the big white tent erected on the Bruce Embankment, second shots had been played, and the players were heading for the bridge across the Swilken Burn.

'Ready, sir?' Jimmy Alexander, the starter, asked.

'Yes. Absolutely,' Hector replied. Fishburne nodded.

'Match number five. Sheriff H.N. Drummond, Royal and Ancient, against Captain L.P.G. Fishburne, Royal and Ancient. Play away, please.' There was more than a hint of the parade ground about the announcement. A few spectators stood still and looked towards the tee.

Willing his hand not to shake, Hector teed up his ball and went to get his driver from Tommy.

'Full shoulder turn, sir, and you'll be fine.' His caddie's encouraging grin banished some of his fear. He had played from this tee hundreds of times; his target was the widest fairway in the world; he could tell Fishburne was scared too. One slow practice swing and the moment had come. Self-consciously, he twisted his hips as Jones did and immediately started his backswing.

His eyes, permanently damaged by mustard gas, could not see the ball finish, but the solid click at impact and Tommy's 'Good shot, sir,' told him all he needed to know. He kept a poker face though inside he was ecstatic. Taking several flicks to coax a flame from his lighter, he lit a cigarette and drew the smoke deep into his lungs.

Fishburne's drive was competent, but several yards short of Hector's. His second, half-topped, pitched short of the Swilken and seemed bound for the water, but, with outrageous good fortune, skipped over the burn and finished close to the hole.

'Never mind him, sir. He'll no' get away with that all day. Nice and easy, now.' Tommy handed Hector his mashie-niblick.

Again, Hector swung well, but the following breeze caught the ball and it rolled to the back of the green. His long approach putt was five feet short.

Using a curious implement that resembled a lump of lead fixed to a walking stick, Fishburne putted for the hole. Over-hit, it would have been six feet past had it not hit the back of the hole, jumped in the air, then disappeared. A birdie.

'Good putt,' Hector muttered, feeling as if he had been punched in the stomach.

Fishburne's drive at the second was safe, but Hector cut his, finishing in the rough grass on the right. He was lucky to have missed the whin bushes, a prickly, yellow ribbon between the Old Course and its neighbour, the New.

'It's not a bad lie,' he said to Tommy. 'I can reach the green with a mashie.'

'A five is often good for a half here,' Tommy said, his hand on the niblick.

Hector was not for wavering. Swinging his mashie with all his might, he struck the ball with the neck of the club, where the blade met the shaft. The ball squirted forty-five degrees off-line, deep into the whins. Cursing under his breath, Hector found a path into the bushes and began a search he knew to be as hopeless as it was uncomfortable.

'Sheriff Drummond, sir. Sheriff Drummond!' Tommy did not sound as if he had found the ball.

The whins had been there for many years and grew densely, up to seven feet in height. Although Hector was not far from his caddie, it took time to reach him.

Tommy was standing in a grassy clearing. In front of him, a man lay on his back, his straight legs forming a perfect V. Above polished brown brogues and beige kilt stockings, his knees and thighs were bare, blanched and puny-looking. His modesty protected by brief green shorts, a red and yellow kilt had been drawn up to his neck, its hem blood-stained. The grass round his head had been soaked in blood. There was a gaping wound in his scrawny neck. Dried blood formed a crust on his upper lip. From the ground beside his head protruded the handle of a *skean dubh*.

'Oh God,' Hector exclaimed. He bent over to make sure but he knew that face. The glazed, staring eyes belonged to Gordon Macmillan, Sorley's father. Hector had last seen him when they had a tense conversation concerning the two expulsions from Glenalmond.

Hector straightened up. He looked round the clearing, collecting his thoughts. The side of one bush was dead, leaving gnarled, twisted branches exposed. On the carpet of brown thorns and twigs, deep within the bush, a bottle lay on its side. The distinctive white label caught Hector's eye. It was Warre's Port.

Without thinking, Hector reached into the bush and picked up the bottle, which contained a small amount of liquid. The label revealed it to be the 1904 vintage. He stared at it, horribly afraid that it might have come from his house, and sniffed. The rich bouquet that filled his nostrils made his heart sink. Had the bottle lain there long, the port would have turned to vinegar. He realized that his fingerprints were on it and put it back, aware that Tommy was looking curiously at him.

'Have you got it, Hector?' Fishburne's voice came from the fairway.

'No, Laurence.'

'Shall I let the match behind through?'

'Yes, do.' Hector made his way to the fairway, Tommy

behind him. Hector turned to face his caddie, shaking his head. 'It's over, Tommy. I can't go on after that.'

'No, sir. I dinnae feel too good either.'

'Your match, Laurence,' Hector said, extending his hand. 'We've just found a murdered man in the bushes. I'll have to give you a walkover.'

*   *   *

Alone in the clearing with the dead man, the others having gone back to report, Hector's thoughts were black. Gordon Macmillan had been a nuisance while alive. Now he was a bigger nuisance dead. Pinch-faced, teetotal and a prominent member of St Andrew's Episcopal Church, he had been free in his criticism of others yet quick to take offence. It had been said about him that to be a good Christian he must have had a lot of faith and hope, because there was not an ounce of charity in him. Disapproving of the socially down-market All Saints' Church allowing their hall to be used for drama, his snide comments had distressed a number of those involved in Lavender's production, which he had called "the school play". Although he was a solicitor, he had been a man of business rather than a court practitioner. There had been one acrimonious exchange concerning the validity of a will soon after Hector had arrived in Cupar to serve as the local judge. After that the two men had few dealings.

When Sorley and Jake were expelled Macmillan had been quick to pin all the blame on Jake, telling anyone who would listen that 'young Drummond' was undisciplined, dissolute and a bad influence. He had asked to meet Hector, hoping to persuade him to intercede with the school on Sorley's behalf, but his self-righteous tone had provoked a warmer defence of Jake than Hector might otherwise have given.

Looking down on the repellent corpse, Hector reflected that it was typical of Gordon Macmillan that he should have spoiled the Amateur Championship. If only he had taken Tommy's advice and used a niblick for his second, he would be playing the third, two down probably, but a good deal happier.

Tentatively, he felt the right arm. It was stiff, cold, and covered in dew. The bottle worried him; 1904 had been an outstanding vintage. He would not be the only man in St Andrews to have some in his cellar. And yet … He was relieved that Jake had spent the previous day and evening at home.

Swinging his arms against the cold, he looked round the clearing. The grass had been flattened, as if people had sat there. He counted five cigarette ends, three smoked down to near the end, wasting nothing, two barely half-smoked. He also saw some spent matches. In a bush close by Macmillan's head, he spotted a curved object, paler than the yellow blossom around it. He stepped carefully, avoiding the blood, and managed to see that the thing was made of horn with an intricately-crafted design. Briefly he hesitated, then pulled, careful not to let his fingertips touch it. The object was a shepherd's crook, over four feet of sturdy wood. It had been thrust lengthways into the dense, tangled branches of the whin. Hector could see no blood on it, and he did not recognise it. He heard no-one approaching. Gripping the horn handle over the handkerchief he wrapped round it, he prodded the port bottle further into the undergrowth, turning it till the label was hidden. Carefully, he slid the crook back into its original position.

At length, Hector heard Tommy's voice. With him came Sergeant McNeill, red-faced, out of breath and sweating, and young PC Gemmell, who, in Hector's estimation, had ninety per cent of the St Andrews force's combined brainpower. After giving them the basic details of the unhappy find, Hector and

Tommy trudged back to the clubhouse, more downcast than after a heavy defeat.

*   *   *

'Have you taken a bottle of port?' Hector tried to keep his voice even as he swung Jake's bedroom door open.

'Sorry, Papa?' There was more than a hint of insolence in the boy's voice as he looked up from his book, an exaggerated expression of innocence on his round face.

Hector held his temper in check. He looked down at his step-son, his tall frame stretched on the bed, his right hand brushing dark hair back from his face in a gesture Hector recognized; John had done that when he was worried. Hector noticed bruising on the knuckles.

He spoke slowly. 'The Warre's 1904. There was a bottle in the pantry yesterday.'

A strange look passed over Jake's face and his shoulders relaxed. 'I assumed you wanted it decanted, so I did that. I can't revise all the time, and I quite enjoy a little butling.'

'I didn't see it ...'

'On the shelf on the left as you go in. I'd love to try it. I didn't get any after lunch yesterday, don't you know?' He put on a pleading smile. 'How did your golf go? You're back early.'

'What happened to your knuckles?' Hector asked sharply.

'Moving the castle wall between scenes.' Jake put on a puzzled expression. 'Why? And what happened to your match?'

Hector sighed as he pulled a chair back from the table strewn with jotters and textbooks. On returning home, he had gone straight to the pantry and found the bottle he had left there missing. Glad that Lavender was out at a rehearsal, he had gone to Jake's room, full of anger and apprehension. Hoping he was being told the truth, he sat still for a moment then chose his words carefully.

'Our match couldn't continue. Jake, your friend Sorley's father is dead. We found his body.'

'Dead? Mr Macmillan?' Jake looked genuinely horrified.

'I'm afraid so.'

'Where, how did you find him?'

'In the whins beside the second.' Hector closely watched the boy's face, and saw his mouth twitch. 'Do you know anything about how he might have got there?'

'No.' Jake looked appalled. 'Why should I?'

'There was a bottle of port beside the body. Warre's 1904. Jake, if you know anything at all about this, please tell me. This isn't naughty boys getting kicked out of school. This is murder.'

'Murder?'

'Yes.'

Jake swung round to the edge of the bed. 'I can't take this in. Mr Macmillan dead. What killed him?'

'He had his throat cut. A horrid sight.'

'His throat cut.' Jake's face lost its colour. Hector hoped he was not about to be sick.

'And you were in your room studying last night, as we thought, not sneaking out to meet your friend and share a bottle of port?'

'I was here all night.'

'Good, Jake. You see, I have to be sure.'

'I know, Papa.' He ran his fingers through his hair. 'What happened to your match?'

'After finding the body, neither Tommy nor I felt like continuing, so I gave Fishburne a walkover.' He smiled weakly then left the room.

*   *   *

'You do believe Jake?' As soon as Lavender had parked her bicycle, Hector had taken her into the drawing room, where they would be alone, and told her everything.

'He's probably telling the truth. There is a decanter of port in the pantry, as he said, and I think it's Warre's 1904, but I can't be sure.'

'You doubted him enough to taste it?'

'Well, yes. Darling, if he was anywhere nearby when Macmillan was killed, the sooner we know the better. For his sake.' Faced with Lavender's bleak look, he drained his sherry and lit a cigarette. 'How did your rehearsal go?'

'All right, I suppose. It was just for me, ahead of the dress rehearsal tonight. Alex Paterson wants me to be really evil, and I don't know if my acting's up to it.' She clasped and unclasped her hands. 'He said I was better this morning.'

'Good. Darling, you'll be wonderful.'

'It's easy for you to say that. How do you sleep-walk across a stage, distraught and rotten to the core at the same time?' She looked down at her hands and placed them flat on her knee. 'Have you told the girls?'

'I said Mr Macmillan died. They didn't seem much bothered. Of course, they didn't know him. They keep on about a half-term treat.'

'I wish this wasn't half term. Could you do something with them this afternoon?'

'Of course.' Hector had hoped to watch Jones play later, but he could see Lavender badly needed his help.

*   *   *

'Maybe Papa will take you to the beach for a donkey ride then ice cream,' Lavender said.

'Please, Papa, please,' Marie and Charlotte cried in unison.

Lunch had been a melancholy affair with little conversation. Now they were finishing their puddings.

'What did you do this morning?' Hector asked the girls.

'We played hide and seek. Indoors. Then Mrs Alves sent us out when the sun began to shine. I fell on the gravel. Look.' Charlotte stood up and pointed to a red mark on her knee.

'It looks as if Mrs Alves has dealt with it very well,' Hector said after inspecting the injury.

'It was more fun hiding indoors. I can be quiet as a mouse, and no-one knows where I am.' Marie chirped.

'What's a spy, Papa?' Charlotte asked.

'Why would you want to know that?' Hector asked.

'Marie says she's going to be one when she grows up.' Charlotte looked round and saw her sister's frown.

'If she grows up,' Jake said quickly, then scraped his plate noisily. He had spoken least of all, and heads turned towards him.

'I'm jolly good at keeping secrets, Jake, and that's what spies do, isn't it, Papa?' Marie hit back.

'That's the most important bit about being a spy. But you have to be able to find out secrets, too.' Hector beamed at his elder daughter. He knew she was clever, and suspected that, in fifteen years' time, women of ability would have an easier furrow to plough than their mothers.

'May I get down, Mama? Papa, please will you take us for donkey rides?' Charlotte already had a winning smile, and knew it.

'Any chance of some port with coffee before you go?' Jake asked innocently.

*   *   *

After an abstemious lunch, the delicate red nectar tasted good. It could well be the Warre's 1904. As Hector savoured his second glass, things did not seem as bad as they had earlier. Jones was not due to start till late in the afternoon. There was plenty of time to treat his daughters to a ride on the donkeys and still see most of the match.

The docile animals, led to the West Sands by their gypsy owners each fine day in summer, would for a penny a ride amble along the beach for a hundred yards or so and back. The beast Charlotte selected remained stubbornly immobile, his sex increasingly obvious. In vain she prodded his flanks with her heels. After several hard whacks from the gypsy's stick, he took off abruptly. This caused Charlotte to shriek and Marie to look superior. The gypsy kept himself between Charlotte's mount and the filly carrying Marie, and the ride passed uneventfully. Both girls smiled happily as the gypsy helped them dismount, his wife grasping the bridle of Charlotte's animal.

'What was wrong with Charlotte's donkey, Papa?' Marie asked.

'He was being awkward,' Hector replied, knowing this would be inadequate.

'There was something funny between his back legs.'

'What do you mean?' Charlotte asked.

'You couldn't see …' Marie giggled.

'I'm sure he'll be fine again tomorrow.' Hector said quickly. 'Come on, let's go and get ice cream.'

'But what …?'

'Never mind. Do you want ice cream – or not?'

The girls understood the emphasis he had placed on the last two words and fell silent. Reminding them that it was a special treat, Hector let them eat their cones in the back of his Bullnose. This kept them quiet as he drove out the Strathkinness road, home to Ballochmyle. After entrusting them to Mrs Alves, Hector checked his leather upholstery for spillage and set off once more for the links.

Parking at the Eden course, he went to the wooden bridge that crossed the railway. From there he could see a great mass of people by the fourth tee. The first time he had come to St Andrews, Jones had torn up his card after bunker trouble on the eleventh. When he had come to play in the 1927 Open, the locals were unsure of him, but by the end of the week he had won them over so completely that he was carried shoulder-high from the last green. Never had there been such a popular champion and people flocked to see him so that they might tell their children and grandchildren that they had seen Bobby Jones play golf at St Andrews. Their affection was reciprocated. Jones had come to love the town, its citizens and, most of all, the Old Course itself. Laid out by God, its quirks and eccentricities both charmed and tested him. After lunch the previous day, he had told Hector that he saw the course as a wise old lady, whimsically tolerant of his impatience but ready to reveal the secrets of her complex being if he took the trouble to study and to learn. Hector had never before heard anyone attribute human characteristics to a golf course. It showed him how much deep thought and imagination Jones put into his golf.

This afternoon, Hector had timed things perfectly. It was a short walk to where the players would hit their seconds. Jones' drive had run into Cottage bunker, some hundred and thirty yards from the green. Hector had heard that the shafts of Jones' clubs had been whittled down to make them unusually whippy and that Spalding had selected balls for him by bouncing them off a hard surface, but this had been an absolutely massive blow. As the crowd jostled for a view, Hector sensed great excitement. Could young Mr Roper be beating the favourite?

Jones was tense and sharp-eyed as he climbed into the bunker. It was hard for Hector to believe this was the same man who had been so relaxed at his lunch table the previous day. Beside Hector, a man wearing a flat cap brought his camera out of its leather case and prepared to snap.

'Please don't make a picture just now,' Jones asked.

Embarrassed, the man stuffed his machine back in its case. Before the clasp was fastened, Jones swung powerfully and the ball sailed over the turf wall towards the green. The applause from those round the bunker was soon deafened by the shouts ahead. They could mean only one thing: he had holed out in two.

'He's level threes now,' a man beside Hector whispered. 'The man's a witch. They ought to burn him at the stake.'

Another said, 'I came eight thousand miles to see this tournament, and that shot is worth the trip.'

The man with the camera cursed under his breath. It would have been a fabulous picture.

With both players producing excellent golf, the crowd of about three thousand were gripped by the contest. On the tenth, Hector felt a hand on his elbow. It was O.B.

'I heard about your bad luck this morning, Hector. What a shame.'

'I couldn't have played on. One of these things, I suppose. This is some match.'

'Bob's gone out in thirty-three and he's only two up. Roper

would be beating anyone else in the field.' O.B. looked very worried.

'Roper looks quite composed. He can't have played in front of a scrum like this before,' Hector said.

'On the second Norman Boase told him not to hurry and to wait until the spectators were out of his way.' Boase was the respected Chairman of the Championship Committee. 'Now he looks as if he has been playing in front of a gallery for years. I don't like it, Hector. This could go horribly wrong.'

*   *   *

'Did you ever see a chap stick the way he did? I knew I was in trouble on the first tee,' Jones confided. He had been four under fours when he defeated the gallant ex-coal miner from Nottingham, three up and two to play. Now he relaxed in the lounge of the Grand Hotel with Mary, Eleanor, O.B. and Hector.

'He had a very clear, steady look in his eyes, and his swing seemed polished and compact,' he continued. 'I guessed he could play and compete under pressure. I was five under par after five. He didn't turn a whisker and I was only three up. If I hadn't been on top of my game, we'd have been in Paris earlier than planned.' He smiled at Mary.

She took his hand. 'Just so long as we get there, Bob. I can wait till after the final.'

'I hear there's been a murder, Hector,' Bob said, turning serious.

''Fraid so.' Hector described his grisly find in the bushes but did not mention the dead man's connections with his family.

*   *   *

'I went to see Lucy Macmillan this afternoon,' Lavender told Hector as they sipped pre-bedtime glasses of port in the drawing room. The dress rehearsal had gone unexpectedly well, Jake had gone to his room and they were alone.

'Oh? I thought you were going to rest.'

'I needed to get out, forget the play for a bit. Long before that nonsense over Glenalmond blew up, Lucy and I met playing bridge from time to time. I've always quite liked her. She's a gentle soul.'

'I've heard he was as ghastly at the bridge table as he was the rest of the time, beastly to his partner if they made a mistake. Can't have been easy to live with. She always struck me as being a bit insipid.'

'She was always better away from him, but now she's devastated. In shock really. I stayed for a bit, took her some lily-of-the-valley. She was very grateful.' She paused. 'I said that we would help her if we could.'

Hector stiffened. 'Right. Did you see young Sorley?'

'He was with his mother. Very attentive, I have to admit.'

Hector knew she had taken a dislike to Jake's friend. 'How did he seem, about his father I mean?'

'Definitely not as upset as she was. He may have been keeping a stiff upper lip, but he spoke of "my father's death" with less emotion than most people speak of the Stock Market Crash.'

Hector looked at her sharply. 'You really don't care for him, do you?'

'There's something sleekit about him, I think, sly, unreliable.'

He shrugged. 'Well he seems to be Jake's best friend these days. Did you learn anything about the murder?'

'Gordon went out for a walk just after half past eight. He was seen by a group of men putting on the Himalayas.'

'At that time of night?'

'There had been a dinner. Someone saw him near the second tee of the Old, and there was some shouting, but the *haar* came in and they stopped their game. Lucy didn't want to talk about it. She and Sorley were in all evening,' she added, glancing meaningfully at Hector.

'When did they report him as being missing?'

'They were about to when they got the news. She said Sorley went to his room after supper. He told her he had gone to bed about ten after revising for his exams. Lucy had a migraine and went to bed about eight. When she woke in the morning Gordon wasn't there but she assumed he had slept in the spare room and left for work without disturbing her. It was when his office telephoned to ask where he was that she got worried. The police got the information about him going for a walk from one of the men putting on the Himalayas.'

She sipped her port then said more brightly, 'Of course, they're lucky with their neighbours, the Moncurs. Doris loves a crisis. She was in and out, organising everything she could, and Willie is such a sweet fellow, really.'

'Totally under her thumb,' Hector said. He had mixed feelings about the Moncurs, who were brother and sister. Their father and grandfather had been respected family doctors in St Andrews. But it was the sister, not the brother, who had followed them. Hector found Doris too loud and bossy, although he would concede she had a heart of gold. 'Needs a man' was often whispered behind her expansive backside. It was said that there had once been such a man, but he had been killed in the last hours of the War, between the signing of the Armistice and the cessation of hostilities.

Willie, four years Doris' junior, was quite different to his sister, in looks, abilities and personality. He could neither read nor write. Letters and numbers appeared to him in unfathomable jumbles. As a child he had endured extra tuition and smacks, but neither had brought him anywhere near the standard of his contemporaries. Unable to get into Merchiston where his father had been, or any other public school, he had gone to a local school that demanded no exam passes. Mocked for his 'posh' accent and apparent stupidity, and picked on for his slight physique, he became handy with his fists, often returning home bruised and sore after painful encounters with other pupils or the teacher's belt. He had left that school at the earliest opportunity, sullen, resentful and lacking in confidence. But he could play golf. It was the only thing he was good at, and he loved every minute spent on the links. After a brief period in the trenches at the end of the War, he became a professional, and taught the game with far more patience than his classroom teachers had ever shown. Now he lived with his formidable sister in the family house in Windmill Road, two minutes' walk from the eighteenth fairway, its drab, unchanged décor a gloomy monument to their dead parents.

'Willie's a damned good golf professional,' Hector said thoughtfully. 'Remember I had a playing lesson from him a couple of years ago? He really got me thinking my way round the course, not always bashing straight at the pin. It's thanks to him I got my handicap down so I could play this week. I know he can't read or write but he doesn't talk like someone who's stupid.' He sighed, lit another cigarette, then shook with a coughing fit that turned his face purple.

'I wish you wouldn't take so many,' Lavender said sharply. 'After the amount of mustard gas you inhaled, your lungs can't stand all the smoke you suck into them. And it's a bad example for Jake.'

'Most doctors smoke.'

'You say that every time, Hector, and it's not right. Doris doesn't, for one.'

'I don't count her.'

'Because she's a woman? She's had to be better than the men to get where she is. I know she's bossy, but if she'd been a shrinking violet, she'd never have become a doctor, and people say she's jolly good at diagnosis. Just think, will you, smoking can't possibly do anything but harm to you.' Her voice caught. 'After John died, when I heard what had happened to you, I thought, not him as well! Every day, I thank God for having you. I want to grow old with you ...' She buried her face in a handkerchief.

Hector cursed himself. He knelt in front of her chair and put his hands on her knee. 'If it's very important to you, I'll stop.'

'When?'

'Now.'

'Really?'

He got up, sat back in his chair, and picked up his cigarette from the ashtray. In silence and inhaling deeply, he smoked until he could no longer hold the butt. Carefully, he stubbed out the final ember and looked at his blackened fingertips.

'That's it,' he said. 'The last one.' Regretting his decision already, he took from his pocket the silver case and the dented lighter that had been John's and placed them on the Dutch marquetry desk by the window. 'Please put these somewhere I won't find them,' he said. 'I'm off to bed.'

5

'There's something you'll have in common with the champion, Sheriff.' Forbes, Hector's bar officer, brought him a cup of tea in his chambers five minutes after his arrival at Cupar Sheriff Court the following day.

Hector looked up, unsmiling.

'You and he will both end the week undefeated.' Forbes chuckled.

'It's not a laughing matter.' Hector felt for his cigarette case. 'Take that damned thing away.' He pushed the grubby stone ashtray across the mahogany table he used as a desk.

Forbes raised his eyebrows. 'Right, Sheriff,' he said stiffly. 'Will that be all, sir?'

The previous afternoon, Hector had telephoned the sheriff clerk to tell him that he should cancel the Honorary Sheriff, as he would be in. The clerk had kept the court diary light during championship week, so the day promised to be easy. As Forbes, unusually monosyllabic, led him on to the bench, Hector told himself not to take out his craving for nicotine on those appearing before him.

His good intentions lasted barely ten minutes. 'Do get to the point, Mr Hotchkiss,' he snapped, as one of the most decent but painstaking of the local solicitors described in minute detail how the loss of his client's job on the railway had led inexorably to a brief and unsuccessful career in housebreaking. As Hotch-kiss failed to trim his plea, Hector scratched his brow in irritation and only just stopped himself from adding to the sentence of three months he had already decided on.

'It's no' easy, giving up the cigarettes,' Forbes said as he helped Hector disrobe later.

'I'll soon get used to not smoking,' Hector replied with more confidence than he felt.

'When my old sergeant gave up he rewarded himself with an extra dram at night. He said looking forward to that made him happier during the day.'

Hector frowned then smiled. 'I might try that.' He tied his tie carefully, making sure it sat properly in the stiff, white collar he wore to court. 'I'm sorry if I was short with you earlier,' he said.

'I didn't notice.' The older man lied.

'I don't suppose you've heard anything from your old friends in the police about the murder?' Forbes, a retired policeman, was usually able to provide Hector with the latest gossip.

'They say Mr Macmillan willnae be missed, sir. The *skean dubh* beside him was definitely the murder weapon. His own, apparently. He'd had a bang on the head, the left temple, too. And a blow to his mouth. He died between eight and ten last night, the doctor says ...' Forbes' voice drifted.

'And?' Hector asked.

'Inspector McTaggart was looking very carefully at the son. I believe he knows your boy, sir.'

Hector scratched his forehead. 'Hmm. Thank you, Forbes. I'll see you tomorrow.' With a sinking feeling in his stomach, Hector drove to St Andrews. A couple of whiskies in the Royal and Ancient lifted his mood slightly as he went out on the course to watch the golf.

*   *   *

'... Come, you spirits

    That tend on mortal thoughts! Unsex me here,

    And fill me from the crown to the toe top full

    Of direst cruelty; make thick my blood ...'

Lavender whispered her speech to the tightly wrapped, round, green buds. A few weeks, and they would be deep red peones. But in five hours she would be stiffening her stage husband's resolve before a human audience, all the more terrifying because she knew them, and they would not forget her performance. Word-perfect, she struggled to sound and appear sinister not absurd, calculating not fantasising, ruthless not blustering. The peones, their backbones straightened by garden canes, nodded gently back. Twisting her hands, Lavender went to sit on the wooden bench that faced south-west, where she had passed so many peaceful summer afternoons, reading, sipping lemon squash and admiring her beloved herbaceous border.

    This afternoon could have been like that, if only ... if only she had said no when they'd offered her the part. No one else had been prepared to take it on, that was the truth, not the stuff about what a wonderful actress she was. It served her right for appearing intelligent and talking about some of the modern plays they might do. How boy actors played the part in Shakespeare's time, she did not know. Maybe they liked the bloodthirstiness. Jake certainly did. It had been good for him to have this interest after Glenalmond. He couldn't swot all the time. He'd wanted his friend, Sorley, to come along as well. They needed as many soldiers, spear-carriers and scene-shifters as they could get, and even Tommy Addison had been persuaded to be an extra. But Gordon Macmillan had put his foot down. She had secretly been quite pleased about that.

Now Macmillan was dead, murdered like King Duncan. Lavender found the intrusion of a real murder into her current world of dramatic murders horribly unsettling. Particularly because of Jake. She hoped against hope that he had not sneaked out on Sunday night. Could he have hidden his tracks by taking a bottle of good port from the pantry and decanting it? She didn't know how many bottles should be there, so she couldn't check. She wondered if Hector had gone to the pantry and counted them. But would he have known how many should be there? She could tell he really didn't trust Jake's word.

But she didn't either. That was the real reason she had visited Lucy Macmillan, and she was only partially reassured. Inspector McTaggart, Hector's *bete noir*, had called shortly after the finding of the body. Lucy admitted that she had found his visit most distressing. He had asked a number of searching questions and even taken fingerprint impressions. Lucy remained affronted but Sorley appeared to be taking the whole thing in his stride. Their contrasting demeanours had given the house an air of unreality. She knew that Gordon had been a strict father, perhaps oppressively so. Had Sorley returned after Jake had left and … The lifting of the kilt demonstrated contempt and dislike for the dead man, something a sleekit person would do. Lavender hoped that McTaggart would identify the right man, or boy, and make an early arrest.

Tonight, tomorrow and Thursday, three performances then she would leave Lady Macbeth on the pages of Shakespeare. She closed her eyes and turned her face to the sun, craving a little peace before her stomach filled with butterflies.

*   *   *

The All Saints' church hall, built after the War with money donated by a Mrs Younger, was spacious. It had folding doors between two areas. The smaller area was three feet higher than the other and, with the doors pushed back, formed an effective stage. Sewn-together bedsheets, suspended from wires and serving as curtains, and a row of footlights behind battered tin shades were not calculated to create confidence in the audience. Hector strode up and down between the rows of chairs and benches trying to look useful. He patted his jacket pocket, feeling for his cigarettes and lighter, and realized he had not thought of smoking for five whole minutes. Forbes' whisky-drinking tip helped, and he had his hip flask in his pocket. He would just have to be careful not to over-do it.

He had seen Lavender to the pantry, now the Green Room, the actors' area, down four steps behind the stage. He hoped that she would not sense how nervous he was. In the car she had been quiet but calm. Jake, meanwhile, had talked non-stop. That morning, the senior pupil at Madras College due to play Young Siward had broken his leg playing football, and Jake had been happy to take the part when the producer had telephoned at lunchtime. It was not a big part, and Jake had gone through it several times on the drive into town. More challenging than the words was the sword-fight with Macbeth. Hector could hear the clack of wooden swords behind the curtain as the actors rehearsed.

But Hector had his own task to learn. He had avoided a part in the play because of the Amateur Championship but, to support Lavender, he had agreed to be in charge of the auditorium, checking that people sat in the right places, and making sure those selling tickets and programmes were doing what they were supposed to. Whatever that was.

Alex Paterson, the producer, emerged from between the

curtains, jumped down from the stage and approached him. Succinctly, he went through the grades of seats, chairs at the front, pews with cushions in the middle, and unpadded benches at the back. He introduced Hector to those dealing with tickets and programmes and, thanking him for his help, rushed out through the side door of the auditorium. This opened onto an open-air passage leading from the street to a paved area at the rear of the building, where there was a door to the Green Room/ pantry. Paterson was taking the best way from the auditorium to the Green Room for those avoiding the jump up to the stage.

Hector did not have long to wait before the first members of the audience drifted in. Five minutes before the start, Bob and Mary Jones arrived with the Keelers. The vagaries of the draw meant that Bob was not required to play that day, and they were all in good humour. There was an excited murmur as Hector showed them to their seats. He put them on the extreme right side of the auditorium, in the second row, where he hoped they would not catch Lavender's eye. Shortly after them came Doris and Willie Moncur, with Lucy and Sorley Macmillan. Lucy was pale and strained while Sorley's jaw was set. It was an expression that made him look like his father. Both avoided eye contact with anyone, Hector included. Wondering why they had come at all, he placed them directly behind the Jones party. Their arrival produced a murmur a few octaves lower than the one that had greeted Jones. As they took their seats, Sidney Roper slipped in unobtrusively and sat on one of the unpadded benches.

By the time the doors closed, the church hall was almost full. The audience included a party of senior girls from St Leonard's School, conspicuous in their beige uniforms. Hector knew that if Jake realized they were there he would over-act horribly.

At half past seven, the auditorium lights went off, the footlights came on then dimmed jerkily. Unseen hands pulled back the curtains then waggled a tin tray to produce stage thunder.

'When shall we three meet again,

In thunder, lightning, or in rain?' the first witch cackled. The show was on.

Sitting uncomfortably at the back, Hector awaited Lavender's entrance with trepidation. When she did come on he momentarily failed to recognize her as she had not told him about the black wig Paterson had borrowed for her from his friend Mrs Savile of Perth Theatre. Reading out a letter, she spoke clearly and loudly. Then she put the letter aside and delivered a long speech with an intensity that emphasised the vileness of the treacherous plan she had formed. At the interval, which Hector called "half time", it was clear from the applause that the evening was going well. He slipped back-stage to tell Lavender, and found her talking earnestly to Banquo, fresh from his appearance as a ghost, and smeared generously with white make-up and stage blood.

'Darling, Alan is worried about tomorrow. He's going to see the police.' In real life, 'the blood-bolter'd Banquo' was Alan Corbett, a sturdy local farmer and town councillor. When Hector moved closer to her, she whispered, 'He was out on Sunday night and thinks he saw the murderer.'

Hector was taken aback. 'Oh. I'm not sure I can help much.'

'Well, I'd like some advice … I thought you'd be the best man to ask.' His make-up gave his face, creased with worry, a sinister look.

'Mama, look! I'm a future king of Scotland!' Wearing a crown, Jake rushed over and affected an arrogant pose.

'Could I see you afterwards?' Hector said to Corbett as Jake listed the role changes he was about to perform.

'Five minutes!' Paterson's voice sounded over the buzz of conversation.

'I'd better go and check the audience,' Hector said. He put an arm round Lavender's waist. 'You're superb,' he whispered.

Jake said, 'Papa, I see Sorley and his mother are here. Could you invite them to the party afterwards? They're obviously trying to put a good face on things.'

'Lucy told me she wants to build bridges as soon as possible. They can always say no,' Lavender said.

Hector nodded then resumed his front-of-house duties, asking the audience to resume their seats. He spotted the Macmillans and the Moncurs, and, taking a deep breath, approached them.

'I was so sorry to hear …,' he said. 'Em, the cast would be very happy if you would all join them and some of the audience for a glass of wine when the play's finished. Just hang around at the end, if you want to. Of course, we'll understand if …'

'Thank you, Sheriff Drummond. We'd be delighted.' Lucy Macmillan spoke softly, with no emotion.

'Good, good. Jake will be pleased to see you, Sorley.'

Sorley smiled. 'Thank you very much, sir,' he said. He put a protective arm round his mother as they moved along the row to their seats. He certainly appeared to be looking after her, whatever Lavender thought of him.

Two uncurtained windows high on the walls prevented the church hall from being effectively darkened, but when the lights were switched off and the footlights came on, the audience fell silent again. Lavender was left with only the famous sleep-walking, hand-washing scene. Clad in a long-sleeved flannelette nighty with a lace collar Hector knew well, she executed it with a haunting tremor in her voice. Jake's big moments came near the end of the play. Obviously enjoying himself, he murdered and was killed flamboyantly. As the final curtain came down, prolonged applause resolved any lingering doubts about the project.

'Excellent, Hector, excellent,' Bob Jones said as he left. With an early start the next day, he had turned down the invitation to stay for drinks.

'Tell Lavender she was wonderful,' Mary enthused. 'It was a great way to spend an evening. I wish we could join you, but O.B. and Eleanor will tell us about it.' Hector looked over to where the Keelers were chatting to Roper.

'Margaret! Now!' With a face and voice that had struck terror into thousands of schoolgirls, the mistress accompanying the St Leonard's party called a willowy, hazel-eyed girl to whom Sorley was talking earnestly. A look combining dislike and contempt flitted across the girl's face before she obeyed, her right hand trailing as Sorley held on to it. Hector could tell from the battleaxe's raised eyebrows that any trouble the girl was already in had just got worse.

After most of those not invited to the party had filed out, Paterson shut the main door. Chairs and benches were pushed aside and trestle tables were brought out and erected. Soon they were stacked with glasses, bottles and plates of scones.

'You're welcome to stay, Mr Roper,' Hector said, noticing a look of mild concern on the former coal miner's face. 'Unscrew a bottle of beer and enjoy yourself.' Roper's forced smile showed he did not like being patronized.

The sole discordant note had come from Fiona Torkington, who commented loudly about an amateur production for the Amateur Championship. Freddie, her husband, looked embarrassed but Hector noted that they were in no hurry to leave.

By contrast, the cast members' excitement was palpable. A week earlier triumph had seemed a long way off. Still in their costumes, they mixed with their guests, basking in their compliments. In one corner, Jake and Sorley spoke, their faces serious, their glasses full. Lavender was with Lucy. Hector discussed the Amateur with Willie Moncur. Tommy, who had looked horribly self-conscious on stage, was laughing with fellow extras, a wine bottle in one hand and a nearly empty glass in the other.

Seeing Alan Corbett hanging about nearby, Hector excused himself from Willie and went over to him.

'It's silly, I know, but I don't know what to tell the police,' Alan said, causing heads nearby to turn. Like many, including Hector, he had returned from the War deafened by shellfire, and did not always pitch his voice at an appropriate volume.

'You should tell them everything you know that might be relevant,' Hector said.

'I'm not totally sure, but I may have seen the murderer. Memory's a damn funny thing.'

'It can be.'

'Sometimes there's an image that you can't get out of your head. Know what I mean?' Corbett took his arm and led him to the side of the hall, away from other people. He spoke in a confidential bellow. 'On Sunday I was at a pre-championship dinner at the New Club. It was for men who live nearby and have played in the Amateur in the past. We call ourselves "The Pams". There were about a dozen of us. Some of us piled out about half past eight and went to putt on the Himalayas. All a bit squiffy and dressed for dinner. No pins in the holes when we got there of course, but we had some fun till the *haar* came in. About the time it became really thick, I saw Gordon Macmillan crossing the Swilken. Miserable looking, as usual. You know that red and yellow kilt he wore? Then there was shouting from the direction of the second on the Old. Male voices.' He dropped his voice. 'A bit later I saw someone else, walking. We were going back to the club for a nightcap but I saw this person near the eighteenth tee through the *haar*. But you know how *haar* makes shapes look different? I'd hate to make a mistake, get someone into trouble. What should I say?'

'You should tell the police you're not sure, and give them as many details as you can remember.'

'We shouldn't really have been on the Himalayas, and the car wobbled about the road on the way home. D'you think they'll worry about that? Will I be charged with drunk driving? It wouldn't do for me, you know.'

'You might get a lecture, I suppose, but they couldn't do anything about the driving now, and it doesn't matter beside a murder.'

'Oh, thank you, Hector.' Looking relieved, he headed back into the throng. 'I loathed sneaks at school, you know,' he added.

'We all did, I think.'

'Never liked seeing chaps get into trouble.' He poured himself another glass of wine. 'Quite a decent little Beaujolais, don't you think? While the green room's quiet, I'll go and get this muck off my face and out of my hair – what's left of it.' Hector smiled. The farmer, losing his grey hair and normally ruddy-cheeked, had made a robust Banquo, probably not unlike a genuine medieval Scottish nobleman.

Not all of those enjoying the hospitality had been invited. Telling themselves this had been an oversight; they had lingered behind after the final curtain and, like Roper and the Torkingtons, had been made welcome. If they spread the word that the play was good, they were worth a glass or two. The scones, baked by the third witch earlier that day, and containing no;

'Liver of blaspheming Jew,

Gall of goat, and slips of yew'

or other esoteric ingredient, were soon devoured. There was nothing else with which to soak up the drink, and the noise level rose. A few slipped out of the main door at the back of the hall. Alex Paterson stood on a chair to make a short, witty speech, thanking everyone. When he finished, more drink was poured and the general noise began to rise again.

The happy atmosphere was shattered by a metallic crash then a scream from behind the stage. Everyone turned to see the third witch, still in costume, emerge from behind the back curtain. She held up both hands, which were covered in red liquid, and uttered a shriek full of real horror. 'Banquo ... Alan ... dead,' she gasped.

Hector knew the rest looked to him. He took a deep breath and clambered on to the stage then pushed the back curtain aside and went down the four steps and through the door leading to the Green Room. The first impression was of a changing room. All around were clothes; some piled haphazardly, others folded neatly. Above the sink a large mirror had been propped and tubes of grease paint lay in front of it. On the far wall to his right was a basin, smaller than the sink. In front of it was a chair. Lolling in it, his head thrown back, Alan Corbett's eyes stared at the ceiling. Hector moved closer and saw the white make-up had been cleaned from his face but red paint still discoloured his hair. His tunic was also stained red. It had not been like that ten minutes earlier. This new red was lighter than the stage blood, less viscous, and more plentiful. It stained the white towel draped over his right shoulder. Half hidden by that, the hilt of a dagger protruded from his neck. Blood had spurted from his neck, creating a spatter of bloodstains on the wall in front of him. The water in the basin was dyed red, but the source of that redness could only be guessed at. On the edge of the basin an innocent glass of Beaujolais, the dead man's last drink, sat half-empty.

Hector stood, shocked. The room behind him filled up. 'We need a doctor,' Hector gasped, 'Fetch Doris Moncur.'

The actor playing Macduff left by the door to the stage, returning with the doctor through the external door from the bins area. Doris Moncur, formidable in a heather-coloured tweed suit, looked at the body and grimaced. Ignoring the blood, she felt his neck for a pulse then shook her head. 'He's definitely dead,' she said, her usual stentorian tone softened. Rubbing his forehead, as he did at moments of stress, Hector turned to Alex Paterson. As steadily as he could he said, 'Is there a telephone? We must summon the police, and no-one should leave the building. Banquo ... Alan has definitely been murdered.'

'He was a damned fine actor,' O.B. said to Hector amid the panic and excitement that followed. 'When he took Macbeth's seat at the banquet, and Macbeth said:

"Thou canst not say I did it: never shake thy gory locks at me"

I could have sworn he was looking past Macbeth at me, and he sure made a mean-looking ghost. It would be great if he could come back as a real ghost and finger whoever did this.'

'We'll just have to rely on the local constabulary, with all their human failings,' Hector replied, his lack of confidence detectable from his tone.

*   *   *

Sergeant McNeill poured himself a third, large whisky and sat
back. A difficult day was over and he could relax. The cells were
empty, so no shouting or commotion would spoil his well-de-
served night's sleep. That was the trouble with the police house
in Queens Gardens: he could seldom escape the demands of
the job. On the other side of the fireplace, his wife sat knitting
and talking. He knew that she knew he wasn't listening, but
neither of them cared.

The ring of the telephone jolted him. A healthy swallow,
then he lumbered through to the hall and glared at the blasted
thing.

'Police office,' he announced into the mouthpiece, the
whisky burning his throat.

'Sergeant, it's Sheriff Drummond. I'm at the All Saints'
church hall. There's been a murder. Please come quickly.'

McNeill cursed. 'There's too much of this,' he snapped at
his wife.

Her needles did not falter. 'You're probably right, dear,' she
said soothingly.

*   *   *

Although the police office was only five minutes' walk from the
church hall, nearly half an hour passed before the arrival of
Sergeant McNeill, who smelled of whisky, and PC Gemmell,
who didn't. During that time, Hector, assisted by O.B., Tommy
and Paterson, had secured the building, persuaded everyone to
write down their name and address, and ascertained as best he
could who might have information of value.

'Gemmell didn't answer his telephone,' McNeill blustered

as Hector pointedly looked at his watch. From the red tide that spread across the young constable's face, Hector guessed that he might have been with a girl.

But at least he had come, Hector thought. The situation would have been too much for McNeill sober. In his cups, it was completely beyond him.

'Does Inspector McTaggart know about this?' Hector asked.

'He will be here presently,' McNeill assured him.

That was the answer Hector had feared. He showed the officers the body then, while McNeill spoke to Paterson, Hector took Gemmell aside and explained what had happened.

The near general hysteria following the finding of the body had given way to shock, grief and fear. Everyone realized there was probably a murderer among them. The cast changed out of their costumes quickly and on the stage, using damp towels to wipe their make-up. Small groups formed. People talked quietly, their eyes darting about. If anyone needed the lavatory, which was beside the dead man's basin, they averted their eyes from the corpse.

McNeill was questioning the third witch and Gemmell was with Willie Moncur when Inspector McTaggart arrived. His office lay eight miles away in Cupar, and he lived close to it. Immaculate as ever, his nose wrinkled when McNeill spoke to him. Looking severe, he turned to Gemmell and listened intently, nodding from time to time.

Hector strode up to him. 'Someone should inform the widow as soon as possible, Inspector. My wife and I know her quite well, and I've told Gemmell everything I can. If you have no objection, I'll take my wife, and Jake, of course, and break the news.'

McTaggart stared at him for a moment. 'Very well, Sheriff. I'll know where to find you. Please don't let your wife or your son leave your house before they've been seen by an officer.'

Hector glared but said nothing. Neither man lost an opportunity to score a point off the other, and the last few had been scored by Hector, in court. Now the boot was on the other foot.

6

'And it's his birthday next week.' Jane Corbett dissolved into tears and rocked to and fro, her limbs trembling.

During the War, Hector had written scores of letters to widows, but never before had he broken the devastating news in person. It had taken five minutes to drive to the stone farmhouse on high ground south-east of St Andrews. On either side of the rough track, cattle blinked in the headlights. After what seemed like miles of bends and potholes, the house and outbuildings loomed in front of them, reliably solid against the North Sea winds. Like their dead master. No lights were on. Leaving Jake grumbling in the car, Hector and Lavender felt their way round the side of the house to the front door then paused, dreading what was to follow. The wind caused a gate to swing and creak. Inside the house, a dog barked. The clang of the front door bell made the beast furious. Wishing he had gloves, Hector stood in front of Lavender. A light came on and Jane's voice asked who it was. Hector shouted their names. The wooden front door opened slowly, revealing Jane in a dressing gown, her sharp, brown face lined with anxiety. She held a rope round the neck of a snarling sheepdog and, having clearly seen her visitors, pulled the animal back into a cloakroom.

Now in the sitting room, they sat and watched her agony, unable to say or do anything to lessen her pain. It was a lived-in room, couthy yet classy. The loose covers on the chairs were sun-bleached and worn; carelessly placed glasses had left pale circles on the round mahogany table beside the fireplace; a battered-looking clockwork train set had been shoved into a corner, ready for its next trans-carpet journey.

When Jane fell quiet, Lavender asked, 'What about telling the boys?' Ian and Robert were ages with Marie and Charlotte.

'I'll do it in the morning. I suppose I should keep them off school?'

'That would be better,' Hector said.

Jane sat back on the sofa. 'I can't believe this is happening. When am I going to wake up? I was worried when he was late coming home, but just in case he had an accident. He's been a bit fond of the bottle of late ...'

Hector leaned forward and took her hand. 'This is all real, I'm afraid, my dear. I wish it were not.'

'Do you want me to stay tonight?' Lavender asked softly.

Silently, Jane picked at a loose thread of her dressing gown. 'No,' she said firmly. 'I'm going to have to get used to this. His brother, Martin, isn't far away. When Alan came back from the War, I thought we were going to live forever ...' She dissolved once more. Lavender gave her a handkerchief.

'Did Alan have any enemies?' Hector asked as she recovered.

Jane looked shocked. 'No.'

'Has there been anything at all unusual happening? Has he done anything odd recently?'

'No, no. Who could have done this?' she wailed.

'I wish I knew,' Hector said. 'Did he say anything to you about seeing a person on the course late on the night Gordon Macmillan died?'

'No.' She looked puzzled.

'Are you sure? You see, he was due to speak to the police

tomorrow, and he told me he saw someone but wasn't sure who it was.'

'He was in no state to be sure about anything that night. He hit the byre door, you know, and it's a miracle he got that far without crashing.' Her face twitched.

Before Hector could ask another question, Lavender got to her feet. 'I think we should go now, Jane, if you'll be all right. Get in touch any time. We're so sorry.' She took both Jane's hands in hers.

As they moved towards the door, Hector's attention was caught by a piece of paper on the leather-topped writing desk. It was not a tidy desk; letters and other papers formed haphazard-looking piles. A bit of cheap, lined paper stuck out. It had odd writing scrawled on it. He wondered if it was Greek. As he peered to see better, Jane's arm brushed the pile, obscuring the paper.

'Thank you both for coming,' she said, her voice catching. 'It was better to hear this from friends.' From the door behind which the sheepdog had been shoved came whimpering. She turned and the hall light briefly shone on her stark, hollow-eyed expression. 'He senses it,' she added.

When they reached the car, Jake was lying across the back seat, his mouth gaping. For a moment, Lavender feared he had been attacked. Then she heard the snoring.

*   *   *

They'd let themselves in quietly then watched Jake stumble upstairs to bed. They sat on the sofa in their sitting room, much cleaner and neater than the one they had left, nursing whiskies; Hector's arm round Lavender's shoulder. He ran his finger along one of her eyebrows, still dark from make-up.

'They'll have to cancel. I certainly couldn't do it now. That play must be cursed,' she said, cuddling in to him.

'What a shame, just one performance after all that work,' he said. 'You were a terrific Lady Macbeth, old girl.'

'Do you think the two murders are connected?' Lavender asked.

'Maybe Alan saw the killer on the golf course. Otherwise I can't se a link. I just hope McTaggart gets things right this time. By the way, where did that dagger come from? Do you know?'

'Alex Paterson persuaded Freddie Torkington to lend us a couple of real daggers for the murderers in the play. He has a small collection. He actually offered to lend us swords as well, but Alex thought we should use wooden ones, as there are some fight scenes. The daggers would have been lying around in the green room.'

The insistent ringing of the front door bell startled them. Apprehensively, Hector answered. Standing on the doorstep, shifting from one foot to the other was Sergeant McNeill. Behind him stood PC Gemmell.

McNeill spoke: 'I'm sorry to disturb you, Sheriff, but we are here to interview John Taylor-Smith, also known as Jake Drummond.'

'My son,' Hector barked.

'Yes, sir. May we come in?'

'No. He's asleep. You can come back in the morning.'

'Sir, Inspector McTaggart has ordered us to take him to Cupar now.'

'Do you plan to arrest him?'

'We hope it won't come to that, sir. We would like him to assist us with our enquiries. They are cases of murder, sir.'

'Cases of murder?'

'I'm afraid so, sir. Cases. I'm very sorry, sir.'

Thinking as quickly as he could, Hector showed them into the sitting room. 'They've come for Jake. They want to interview him about the murders,' he explained.

Lavender was on her feet. 'My son is only a boy,' she cried. 'Can't you do something?' she rounded on Hector.

Trying not to sound as if he was pleading, Hector said: 'Sergeant, he is only a boy of seventeen. Would it not be fairer, and better all round, for me to bring him to you in the morning? Do you have any evidence against him?'

There was an edge to McNeill's voice. 'We must bring him back with us now, sir. And we were told not to divulge evidence. Inspector McTaggart was very clear indeed, I'm afraid, sir. Wasn't he, Gemmell?'

'I'm sorry, sir, but yes, the inspector was very clear, and we don't want to have to arrest your son here.'

Hector knew he could not stop them. He shook his head at Lavender. 'I shall go upstairs and waken him.'

McNeill spoke again. 'Gemmell must go with you, sir. We shall require to seize the clothes he wore this evening and Sunday evening.'

Awakened by the doorbell, Jake looked terrified when Hector opened his bedroom door and came in with Gemmell. Sounding as calm as he could, Hector told him what was happening. Self-consciously, the boy turned away from them to change out of his pyjamas. Hector saw a purple weal across his right shoulder blade and another across the small of his back. He thought immediately of the shepherd's crook in the whins. The nightmare was getting worse. A sideways glance told him that Gemmell also had observed the marks.

Expressionless, Jake produced the clothes the police wanted, and they went downstairs.

'I shall follow you to Cupar,' Hector said. 'I wish to be present when my son is questioned.'

Tears running down her cheeks, Lavender hugged Jake until McNeill's hand gently pulled him away.

'Just tell them the truth, Jake,' she shouted as they went out to the car. 'We'll be right behind you,' she added.

Hector nodded grimly. It was going to be a very long night. And he was not sure that telling the truth was necessarily in Jake's best interests.

By the time Lavender had made it clear that she intended to come with Hector and they had told Mrs Alves what was happening, they were ten minutes behind the police car. Mindful of the wine and whisky he had drunk, Hector steered the Bullnose carefully along the dark country roads leading to Cupar. They did not speak and Hector felt that Lavender blamed him for not intervening more effectively. When they arrived at the police station, Gemmell showed them into a small room containing two wooden chairs and a shabby, lop-sided table. A single, small window was covered by a sturdy metal grille.

'As I said, I want to be present while Jake is interviewed,' Hector told him.

Avoiding Hector's eye, Gemmell said, 'Inspector McTaggart has already started the interview with Sergeant McNeill. He insisted I should tell you that no one else is to be there unless he says so.'

'Well I insist you go and tell him right now that I have come here to be with my son,' Hector shouted into the young policeman's face.

'He, he said he was not to be disturbed,' Gemmell stammered, his face red.

'Well, if you won't disturb him, I will,' Hector replied, moving towards the door.

Gemmell stood in his way. 'Please don't, Sheriff.'

'Get out of my way, officer.' Hector spoke slowly, with as much menace as he could. He felt his fists clenching.

'Hector! Don't. You'll make matters worse.' Lavender's voice sounded shrill and full of pain.

Gemmell stood his ground, squaring his shoulders. For a moment the two men stared into the other's face. Then, with a snort, Hector turned away.

Gemmell sighed audibly. 'I'm truly sorry, Sheriff. But I'll go and see what the inspector says.' As he left the room he closed the door firmly behind him.

Lavender slumped on to one of the chairs, kneading her hands in her lap. Hector drew the other chair beside her and put his hand on hers, but she pulled them away. Angry and impotent, Hector's eye caught the cheap metal ashtray on the table and wished he could smoke.

Still red-faced, Gemmell returned. 'I'm sorry, Sheriff, but Inspector McTaggart asked me to remind you that it is up to the police whom they allow to be present while interviewing a suspect. Your son is seventeen, sir, and intelligent. You and your wife will be able to see him once the interview is over, which should not be too long now. I shall be just outside, sir. Would either of you like a cup of tea?'

Both refused tea and Gemmell left. 'Unfortunately he's right,' Hector said quietly once the door had been closed. 'I couldn't do any more, darling. I wish I could.'

'It's not your fault, I know,' she replied, patting his hand. 'I just know he needs me and I'm so powerless.'

More than half an hour passed before Gemmell returned, his face twisted with embarrassment. 'If you come with me, I can take you to your son now. I regret to tell you he has been charged with the murders of Gordon Macmillan and Alan

Corbett. We shall hold him in custody here until he appears in court later today.'

Lavender let out an almost bestial howl and began to weep. Hector put his arm round her. 'Give us a moment, will you?' he asked, his voice catching.

Five minutes later they felt able to face Jake. Gemmell led them along a corridor to a room like the one they had left.

'At least we don't have to go to the cells to see him,' Hector whispered.

Hunched over the table, his hand pushing back his hair, Jake appeared drawn and vulnerable. He looked up, his eyes red with tears. 'I'm sorry, Mama,' he blurted out.

Bit by bit, the story came out, Jake swearing that this time it was the truth. He had met Sorley by arrangement in the clearing where the body was found. Because of Gordon Macmillan's antipathy towards him, it had been necessary to meet clandestinely. Jake had promised to bring a bottle and the Warre's 1904 port had been there for the taking. Jake confessed that he owned a bottle opener for such occasions. He had also taken cigarettes and matches. He had opened the bottle and had begun to drink and smoke before Sorley joined him. About this time the *haar* had come in. Thinking it lengthened the odds against their discovery, the two friends had taken turns in swigging from the bottle. They got the fright of their lives when Gordon Macmillan had loomed out of the mist and burst into the clearing, waving his crook.

'He called us "sinful degenerates" and I said we were old enough to live our own lives and he should leave us alone. There was a bit of shouting and he ordered Sorley to go home. As we began to scramble to our feet, I felt this whack across my shoulder then another on my back. He was really angry. "I'm going to give you the thrashing you need," he shouted at me. Well, I was on my feet, facing him, and he wound up for another whack with the crook. I punched him hard. I was aiming for his jaw, but got his mouth. He sort of staggered back, but gripped the crook, ready to come at me again. I bent and picked up the bottle and he caught me one on the hip. It was bloody sore. Well, I hit him on the side of his head. Hard. He went down. He was unconscious but lying on his side, not on his back as the police say, and I never pulled his kilt up. They say I did.

'Anyway, Sorley had run away. I threw the bottle under a bush and shoved the crook into the whins, too. Then I left. I had my bicycle and going up City Road I nearly hit a man on foot. He was crossing the road.'

'What route did you take?' Hector asked.

'Going there, I went down City Road then cut across the Old Course along Granny Clark's Wynd then up to near the first tee of the Jubilee. I left my bike there and walked down to the clearing in the whins. I took the same route coming back. Sorley said he'd come the same way. I don't know how Mr Macmillan knew where to find us. We arranged it on the telephone so I suppose he must have overheard.'

'Has Sorley spoken to the police, do you know?'

'They told me they'd questioned Sorley this evening, and he told them what had happened. I didn't kill him, honestly. But they say I did, then killed Mr Corbett because he had spotted me.' Jake looked from Lavender to Hector. 'Please help me get out of here.'

'Did you tell the inspector all this?' Hector asked, a sinking feeling in his stomach.

'Yes. After they told me what Sorley had said.'

'And before that?'

'I told them what I'd told you,' he whispered miserably.

'Did they write down what you said?'

The boy nodded.

'Both stories?'

He shrugged. 'I think so.'

'Did you sign anything?'

'My statement.'

'And did they read it over to you?'

'Yes, but by then I was only half listening. I couldn't think.'

'Did they tell you at the start that you were not obliged to say anything and that anything you did say could be used against you at your trial?'

'I think so, but the inspector kept asking questions. I was scared. I felt I had to answer.'

'Did they challenge what you said?'

'The inspector kept telling me I'd done it and it would be better for me if I told them the truth. But I was, honestly.' He started to cry.

Lavender, shaking with silent tears, twisted her handkerchief. Hector had never seen Jake so vulnerable. 'What about Alan Corbett? What did you tell them about his case?'

'Just that I'd heard what he told you after the play, that he'd seen someone but didn't want to get them into trouble. But he shouted all the time. Lots of people must have heard too. They told me I'd killed him, but I haven't killed anyone.' He buried his head in his hands and sobbed.

As Lavender put her arms round him, Hector shook his head. The boy had confessed to being at the scene of the crime and fighting with Macmillan, then overhearing a witness say he might identify the killer. The crown would not need much more to obtain a conviction for a double murder. 'As they've charged you with murder, you'll be remanded in custody. We can't do anything about that. But I can get you a good lawyer ...'

'I want Mr Hotchkiss, Papa. I know him and he's always decent, talks to young people as well as …'

'Old people?' Hector finished the sentence. Hotchkiss would not have been his first choice, but it was important to have a solicitor with whom Jake felt comfortable. In any event it would be Senior Counsel who would win or lose the case at trial.

A knock at the door told them their time together was up. Jake hugged his mother as if he never wanted to let go then shook hands with his stepfather.

As they walked through the police station they passed Inspector McTaggart. He looked smug. 'You evil bully,' Lavender hissed. Hector firmly took her arm and led her to the car.

Dawn was breaking as they drove out of Cupar.

In a small voice, Lavender asked, 'They won't hang him, will they?'

'No, he's too young,' Hector said, hoping Jake's youth would save him. But as he was over sixteen he could be hanged, and if he were to be convicted of two murders …

7

'Will Jake get only dry bread and water?' Charlotte asked.

'He'll be given proper food, my dear,' Hector assured her. 'Particularly as he's untried.'

'Innocent,' Lavender spoke for the first time during a fraught, tearful breakfast. Neither she nor Hector had slept after their return from Cupar, and when Hector had broken the news to the girls, their responses were very different: Marie was silent and shocked, while Charlotte wanted to know the gruesome details of Jake's incarceration.

'Will he have to go to the bathroom in a bucket?' her voice squeaked with excitement.

'Possibly,' Hector replied, hoping Lavender would not become more upset.

'Will he have toilet paper?' she continued as she attacked her bacon and egg.

'Not at the table, Charlotte,' Hector said sharply as Lavender rose suddenly and rushed out of the room.

'Mama's upset about Jake,' Hector explained.

As Hector and Marie pushed their food about on their plates, Charlotte finished hers and gulped down her glass of milk. 'May I get down, Papa?' she asked.

'Of course, my dear,' Hector said indulgently. He smiled as he watched her leave the room then turned the smile towards Marie, hoping to reassure her. She sat still, her head down.

'I'm sure things will end up all right,' Hector said, wishing he meant that. 'I'll see Jake later today, as he'll have to appear in front of me.' Jake would have to be brought before a sheriff, and as the remand in custody pending further investigation would be automatic, Hector saw no reason why he should not preside at the brief hearing.

'Please don't be angry, Papa,' Marie whispered.

'What is it? Is this something to do with Jake?'

She nodded.

Hector kept his voice gentle. 'You must tell me. For Jake's sake, I need to know everything.'

'You know the window at the end of the corridor upstairs?'

'Of course. The one with the old Wisteria outside?'

'Yes. That one. Well, on Sunday I pulled it so it looked shut for Jake.'

Hector had wondered how Jake had managed to slip in and out of the house. 'Go on. You must tell me everything. And I promise I won't be cross with you if you do.'

The little girl took a deep breath then a torrent of words flowed out of her. 'You know how Jake went to his room after dinner? He said he was revising, but he wasn't. After you said goodnight to us at half past seven, I told Charlotte I needed the bathroom and went to his room to tell him you and Mama were in the sitting room and Mrs Alves was in her room. He put a pillow under his blanket to make it look as if he was asleep in bed then went downstairs. He came back with a bottle, which he put in his jacket pocket then climbed out of the window. Once he was on the Wisteria I pulled the window so it looked shut but wasn't. He said he couldn't use the front door as you would hear it creak and Mrs Alves sits in her room looking out over the back door. He got out then in again by climbing on the Wisteria. He rode his bike to meet his friend. He promised he'd be back and in bed by ten, and you and Mama never go to bed before half past. I knew it was wrong, but … I'm sorry, Papa.'

'How did he persuade you to help him?'

Marie looked as if she was about to cry. 'He bought me sweeties. Chocolate.'

'Had he ever done this before?'

'Just once, I think. After he was sacked from Glenalmond. I saw him sort of playing with the window as if he was trying to make it look shut. He told me I mustn't tell anyone.'

'And that's all you can tell me?'

'Yes. I went back to bed and fell asleep.'

'Thank you, Marie. And no, I'm not cross with you.' Hector got up and kissed his daughter's head. 'Now I must get ready for court.'

As he spoke, the telephone rang. Mrs Alves, red-eyed, came in. 'It's the sheriff principal for you, sir.'

Hector groaned. There could be only one reason for Crichton Fairweather KC to call and Hector could not bear his grandiloquent pomposity at the best of times. He patted Marie's head and walked slowly to the hall.

'Good morning, Fairweather,' he said, observing the bar convention of using surnames.

'I wish that it were, Drummond. I wish that it were.'

'I suppose you've heard about my son?'

'Indeed; I regret to say that the news reached me at breakfast. Naturally, you have my condolences.'

'Well, thank you …'

'But *filius est pars patris*; the son is a part of the father, as you well know …'

'I did Latin.'

'And *de fide et officio iudicis non recipitur quaestio*. There must be no question regarding the good faith and duty of a judge. For now at least, your position in Cupar is untenable, I regret to say. In this case, the sins of the son are being visited on the father. Unfortunate, of course, but ...'

'Jake is not only presumed to be innocent. He is innocent.'

'Indeed, indeed. However it is my view, my fixed view, that you should not sit as a sheriff until this unhappy matter has been resolved. I intend to catch the first available train north. I shall cross the Forth and take today's court myself. I gather that your son is due to appear, and I would not sanction that appearance to take place before an honorary sheriff. I regret this, Drummond, but remember the wise words of Virgil: *durate et vosmet rebus servate secundis*. Carry on and prepare yourself for better times. Good day to you, Drummond.'

Hector gripped the receiver as if strangling it before slamming it down. 'Damn. Damn and blast it,' he said.

Lavender was in the sitting room, gazing out over the garden.

'That wind is destroying the flowers,' she said sadly.

Hector put his hand on her shoulder and felt her shiver. 'Don't get cold, my love,' he said.

'It's just tiredness. Who was that on the telephone?'

'Fatty Fairweather. I'm not to sit "until this unhappy matter has been resolved". I suppose it would have been Newton, the procurator fiscal, who told him. He's coming through from Edinburgh himself to do Jake's first appearance. I can't stand the way he speaks half the time in Latin then translates what he's just said as if he's talking to an imbecile. I did blasted Latin for nine years at school. He did offer his condolences, but in English, so I'm not sure if he meant it.'

'Will we be able to see Jake?'

'Yes. We can bring him some food and a change of clothes. But first I'm going to telephone Hotchkiss. I would have seen him today at court but a telephone call will have to do. There is one thing you should know, and please don't be cross with Marie ...'

Lavender heard him out, her lips pursed, then shook her head. 'What has got into Jake recently? I want my boy back.'

She got up and from her drawer in the desk brought Hector's cigarette case and lighter. 'I can't ask you to deal with this and give up at the same time,' she said. 'Later, when things are back to normal.'

Hector's fingers handled the familiar, cold metal, recognizing the dents and scrapes on the lighter. 'No,' he said, putting them down. 'I've said I'll do it and I will.'

Lavender kissed him gently on the cheek.

As she busied herself gathering things to bring Jake, Hector spoke to Hotchkiss, who at first was quite monosyllabic. Hector regretted his earlier impatience with him. However, by the end of the conversation they were talking amicably, Hector having impressed on the solicitor that neither expense nor trouble should be spared, and that he wanted to be kept up to date with all developments. To underline his frankness, he divulged what Marie had told him. Finally, mentioning a family connection, he told Hotchkiss that MacGregor Mitchell KC, the unofficial leader of the Scottish criminal bar, should be instructed immediately.

Jake appeared frightened and exhausted when he was taken to see them in the same room as the previous day. It was a stilted, unhappy meeting. Jake seemed pleased about what they had brought, and even smiled when Lavender mentioned toilet paper. Hector asked if he had seen anyone as he left the clearing, but Jake replied that he had just wanted to get away, and could not remember seeing anyone.

'I'm sorry I lied to you at first, Papa, but I thought Mr Mac-millan might not tell anyone as he had attacked me.'

Hector shrugged. He could not bring himself to criticise the boy.

On the way home, Hector, regretting his strong-minded-ness over cigarettes, announced that he intended to find out more about the after-dinner putting on the Himalayas, and the best place to start would be the R and A. He had another rea-son: the luck of the draw had meant that, if both won their morning matches, that afternoon Jones would play Cyril Tolley, probably Britain's finest amateur, and the holder of the trophy, for a place in the last thirty-two of the championship. It had the makings of an epic encounter, and Hector needed respite from Jake's problems.

Striding downhill from The Scores past the Martyrs' Mon-ument to the grey clubhouse, Hector bent his head into a tug-ging west wind that was blowing grains across the West Sands towards the sea. He allowed himself to anticipate what might be a clash of the Titans. Inside the Club, the atmosphere was high. Both Jones and Tolley had survived their morning games, and the match that would have made a perfect final was to take place in the fourth round in the most testing conditions. Armed with a whisky, Hector pushed into the crowded Big Room and found himself beside 'Bean' Hamilton, whose deafness was made worse by the noise level.

'Tell that boy of yours well done,' Bean bellowed. 'Macmil-lan was an excrescence. I hope the beak won't be too hard on him. I gather your boy was defending himself.'

Shocked, Hector thought he should put him right. He took his arm and led him in the direction of the library. Speaking loudly into a large, hairy ear, he briefly explained the situation.

Bean was appalled. 'My dear chap, that's terrible. I don't

suppose they'd … No. If there's anything Esme or I can do, you will let us know, what?'

'Well, I do need to know about a pre-championship dinner at the New Club on Sunday night for men who'd played in the Amateur in the past. I gather some of the fellows went for a late putt on the Himalayas, and one of them might have seen something.' He didn't add, 'or killed Macmillan'.

'Can't help you there, old man. I was confined to barracks on Sunday night, not that I would have been qualified to take part. I can tell you something about Macmillan, though. Just in case it helps. The bounder came to the house unannounced, wanting me to get involved in some investment wheeze he organized. He was buying American stocks as if there was no tomorrow. Said I'd triple my money! That was about three years ago, before the whole caboodle crashed. Of course I didn't touch it with a bargepole. My old housemaster at Eton told me that if something sounds too good to be true, it probably is. I listened politely then showed him out by the tradesman's entrance. He didn't speak to me after that.'

Hector smiled. Bean's family business was jam making. It had been successful in his father's day, and Bean had expanded it profitably. Now retired, he lived with his formidable wife Esme, in a large house a few miles west of St Andrews. His outspokenness had increased with his deafness.

'Thank you, Bean. That's very interesting.'

'Rum sort of solicitor, if you ask me. Mine's in Edinburgh. About a hundred years old and covered in dust, as he should be. But sound. Tell you what, come and have lunch. I'll just pull the Hangman's Dilemma out of the Big Room and he can join us. He was telling us about that dinner on Sunday. You can quiz him over a decent meal and some claret. You look as if you could do with it.'

'The Hangman's Dilemma' was Freddie Torkington's nickname. He had a tiny jawbone, resulting in a chin no bigger than an Adam's apple. If he were to be sent to the gallows, there would be little to stop the rope sliding up over his head. He had been burdened with his unfortunate moniker since schooldays. A fine golfer in his day but now in his late fifties, as he talked about the dinner Hector's eye was drawn to the bizarre way the flesh round his chin wobbled. He imagined a rope round his neck, then thought of Jake …

'…Well, a challenge is a challenge,' Torkington continued. 'So we grabbed putters and balls. You know, I think the best way to deal with the Himalayas is to ignore all the slopes and hollows and just bash it straight at the hole. I was doing quite well too till the blasted *haar* came in. I didn't see anything that would help your boy, but I did hear the shouting. Must have been Macmillan.' His tone changed. Speaking with venom, he added, 'I won't be going to his funeral. Man was a twister and a charlatan.'

Hector had a low opinion of the dead man but he had not heard him denigrated in that way before. 'What do you mean?' he asked.

Torkington's fork quivered over his mince and poached egg, an R and A favourite, before replying. 'He's cost a lot of people in this town a lot of money. Advising them to sell the family silver to buy American stocks. Encouraging them to borrow too. Now look at the mess we're all in. Hmph.' He renewed his attack on his mince and poached egg.

From the way he had been speaking Hector guessed the normally reticent Torkington had spent longer than usual drinking in the Big Room before lunch. 'That's most interesting,' he said, 'Who all was at the dinner?'

Torkington sniffed. 'Enough said about that subject. *Nihil nisi bonum* and all that. Tell me, Hector, who's going to win this afternoon? I know Jones is a good chap, but dammit, Tolley's British. One of us, don't you know?'

'It should be a grand match. That wind will certainly test them.' For all that Tolley was British, a member of the R and A and 'one of us', Hector wanted his friend Jones to win. He had, in previous years, won the Opens on both sides of the Atlantic as well as the American Amateur Championship. The British Amateur was the one major championship he had yet to win. Hector knew that he wanted it very badly. If he did win, he would have the chance to win all four championships in that year, the so-called 'Impregnable Quadrilateral'. Hector glanced out of the window. 'Look, the crowd has almost surrounded the first hole. We'd better get out if we want to see anything.'

'Someone said they'd laid on special trains for people who want to watch this,' Bean Hamilton said.

As Hector had forecast, it was difficult to see the players as they hit their opening drives. A collective gasp told him that one of the drives had been poor. As he followed the scrum down the fairway, Hector hoped that Lavender was bearing up. Perhaps he should be at home with her? He told himself that it was important to show his face boldly, not to be cowed lest he should appear ashamed. That might be taken as an acceptance of Jake's guilt. It was better that he should be seen here, as if circumstances were normal. Was it his imagination, or had one or two men in the Club looked the other way when he was near them? Had the news of Jake's arrest spread like wildfire? As he strained to see the golf he tried to overhear what other spectators whispered to each other.

It was the British player who had topped his opening drive and Jones won the hole with a four. The crowd surged on, elbowing and pushing. Hector was soon separated from Bean and Torkington. He went ahead to the second green and waited there. Tolley won that hole and the match was square. From there to the turn neither player was more than one hole up. Hector knew Jones liked Tolley as well as respecting him, but there could be no question that both men were straining every muscle and nerve to beat his opponent. Of the two, Jones looked the grimmer, his face set, frequently smoking a cigarette as if he was sucking in extra strength. The wind, fierce enough to blow sand from the bunkers, was in their faces going out and made the first seven holes unusually difficult; downwind it was not much easier as neither man could hold the green with his tee shot at the short eighth. The crowd rolled across the links like a tidal wave, forcing the players in the lesser matches to stand over their balls, guarding them from accidental kicks. Able to see perhaps half the shots, Hector was in turn swept along by the general excitement and quietly contemplating his private agony. He kept thinking of what Torkington had said at lunch; *a twister; sell the family silver to buy American stocks; now look at the mess we're all in.* Macmillan had not approached him with his ideas, but that was not surprising, as they had never seen eye to eye.

Coming home, Jones went one up three times before being immediately pulled back to square. Often they had to wait until spectators had been moved by the stewards; Tolley, the bigger man with an aristocratic demeanour, looking American with black and white shoes, perched on a shooting stick; Jones, looking British with a flat cap, sat cross-legged on the ground. They were level when they reached the hazardous seventeenth. Helped by the wind, both men hit long drives over the railway sheds and down the fairway. As the ladies in the crowd tried to shelter from the black coal dust blown from the railway yard, Jones stood on a hillock, assessing his second shot. The green was ringed by spectators, the hole cut far back on the narrow strip between the Road Bunker on the left and the rough, stony road. Like a general marshalling his troops, Jones, helped by the stewards, urged those standing on the left of the green to move back. But they had weaved and barged their way to this advantageous position and were not willing to surrender it. Jones hit his iron shot to the left of the Road Bunker. It bounced then was stopped by a spectator, finishing just over the green and leaving a simple chip. It was not the first time in the match that the spectators had got in the way of a ball. Tolley's iron was poor, the Road Bunker now lying between his ball and the pin. Advantage America. But Jones chipped weakly, leaving himself an eight-foot putt. With the touch of a jeweller, Tolley clipped his ball perfectly. It landed just over the bunker and came to rest two feet from the hole. Advantage Britain. Summoning all his competitive spirit, Jones willed his putt into the hole and Tolley followed him in. It was a half never to be forgotten by those who witnessed it. The eighteenth was halved in four. Each player had gone round in seventy-five in most testing conditions and under the greatest pressure. If the crowd had been made to pay, they would have got their money's worth.

Jones won the nineteenth and the match. He played the hole better then laid Tolley a stymie, his ball blocking his opponent's putt. As Sergeant McNeill and PC Gemmell escorted the victor back to the Grand Hotel, Hector felt a nudge on his elbow. It was Tommy Addison.

'Was that no' the greatest match ever, sir?' he asked.

'I've not seen one better,' Hector agreed. 'Did you see Tolley's pitch at the seventeenth?'

'Aye, sir. Mr Tolley's a magician, right enough.'

On an impulse, Hector said, 'Er, Tommy, would you be good

enough to come and see us this evening? There's something you might help me with.'

'Yes sir. Of course.' Tommy could not keep the apprehension out of his voice. He had heard about Jake's arrest and there was something hesitant about the sheriff's tone of voice. He knew he wasn't going to be asked to mow the lawn.

8

Crouching beside a bush, Tommy wiped his hands on his trousers then put his gloves back on and gripped the jemmy he had borrowed from Ally Drever. It was a warm night but it was nerves that made him sweat. He waited for the moon to go behind a cloud. Though it was well past midnight he never knew who might look out of a window and see him.

When he had arrived at Ballochmyle, the sheriff had ushered him into the posh room he called the drawing room. His eyes were watery and redder than usual and he kept rubbing his forehead. He had begun to talk about Jake and the murders when Mrs Drummond had come in, looking worse than he did, hollow-eyed and pale. Not far from tears, she hadn't liked the sheriff's plan one little bit. 'You don't have to do this,' she had said to the sheriff, then turned to him, put her hand on his arm saying, 'Neither do you, Tommy'. Later she had told the sheriff, 'It's not your fault, you know. I think this is madness.'

Tommy thought it was madness too, but he couldn't say no to the sheriff, who had helped him in so many ways. He remembered the day when he had sentenced him to borstal and then changed his mind. That had been for housebreaking, the one time he had done it and that was three years ago. He hoped he had not lost his touch with a jemmy, but the back window of Mr Macmillan's office looked easy. He was more

worried that the sheriff, waiting as casually as he could outside
the front of the building in Argyle Street, would somehow give
the game away.

Suddenly the night became darker. A cloud had covered
the moon. Tommy waited for his eyes to adjust then moved
carefully towards the window he had selected. He forced the
jemmy into the crack at the bottom then pushed down with all
his strength. With a crack that sounded frighteningly loud, the
window opened. Seconds later, he was inside.

He found himself in an office, quite small, a typewriter
on the desk. No doubt a secretary's room. He pulled the window down, switched on his torch and explored the rest of the
ground floor. He knew it was not a big office, the two floors
above being residential, reached by a close beside the front
door. At the back was a pantry with a lavatory beside it. At
the front there were two rooms, a waiting room and an office
grander than the other with a huge desk, a large bookcase,
an upright wooden cabinet and pictures on the walls. A quick
search failed to reveal the front door key so Tommy opened
the window onto the street. With more agility than Tommy had
expected, the sheriff climbed in, took the torch and, holding a
handkerchief to prevent leaving fingerprints, began to search
the room. Tommy pulled down the blind so the torchlight would
not attract attention.

The cabinet had two drawers, both full of files stored verti-
cally on runners. Hector had never seen one like it. As quickly
as he could, he examined the files in the top drawer, but they
related to run-of-the-mill matters. The files at the back of the
bottom drawer were separated from the rest by a tab labelled
'INVESTMENTS'. Hector whistled under his breath. While
Tommy kept a lookout, he carefully went through them, men-
tally noting names and details. He was astonished at how many

of St Andrews' prominent citizens had taken Macmillan's advice and invested heavily in American stocks. Several of them had borrowed in order to buy more stocks than they could afford. Macmillan had facilitated this, always through the same broker, Harvey W. Feinstein, and the same bank, the Enright Bank of Connecticut. While the stock market had risen the gains had been spectacular, but the Wall Street crash the previous autumn had dramatically changed the picture. With the bank charging compound interest on top of an already high rate, a number of Macmillan's clients were now in debt, some of them substantially.

The files were arranged alphabetically. One related to Alan Corbett. Hector reckoned that he had been insolvent and on the verge of bankruptcy before he died. He wondered if Jane knew the mess she had been left in. The farm would certainly have to be sold. Unless there was life insurance ... no, Jane could have had nothing to do with his death; there had been nothing faked about her grief. He continued to trawl through the files, increasingly astonished that so many men, some clever, a few apparently canny, should have left themselves open to financial disaster. When he reached the letter T, he found a file for Freddie Torkington. His situation was nearly as dire as Corbett's and his file like many, including Corbett's, contained both a letter from Macmillan, regretting the situation but not apologising for his advice, and a letter from the bank requiring early repayment and threatening court proceedings.

The second file from the back related to the Town Council and was thicker than the rest, reflecting the number of investments the councillors had been persuaded to make on behalf of the town. They too had been seduced by greed and had bought shares, then borrowed from the Enright Bank to buy more as if profit had been certain. Considering the rate of interest they were paying on their loans, again compounded, the councillors would have to find hundreds of thousands of pounds to restore the municipal finances.

'I wish you'd hurry up, sir,' Tommy urged, his nerves jangling.

'Just a minute. I have to see this last one,' Hector replied, intent on replacing the Town Council file exactly as he had found it.

As Tommy fidgeted, Hector drew out the last, thin, file. It was labelled 'B Maxwell', a name Hector recognized. It contained only two copy letters sent by Macmillan to Maxwell, who lived in New York. The first, dated 4th March that year, read: 'I refer to our trans-Atlantic telephone conversation of last week. I am grateful to Harvey Feinstein for referring you to me and am now able to respond to your enquiry. With reference to what you call "The Andrean Project", the position is as follows: by Act of Parliament dated 1894 ownership of the Links, formerly held by the Royal and Ancient Golf Club, passed to the Town Council. In exchange for maintaining the Old Course and the Ladies' putting green, members of the Royal and Ancient were accorded significant golfing privileges. Sole charge of the management of the Links was entrusted to a Joint Green Committee, consisting of five members of the Club and two nominees of the Town Council. Further stipulations are that the Old Course must be open to play by members of the public for no charge; it is permitted to charge for play on the New Course; and there is no Sunday golf. As this arrangement was enshrined in Statute, another Act of Parliament would be required to bring about any significant change.'

The last letter in the file was dated three weeks later. Short and to the point, Macmillan wrote that due to the conflict of interest they had discussed in another trans-Atlantic telephone call he would no longer be able to act for Maxwell, but would be happy to recommend other solicitors. The final sentence read: 'I can reassure you that I will continue to respect client confidentiality in relation to your affairs.' A fee note for one hundred and fifty pounds was attached, a hefty sum, Hector thought, for the work involved.

As he thought what implications the letters held, Tommy interrupted him. 'Quick, Sheriff. Out the window. Sergeant McNeill's climbing in the back.' As he spoke, a bellow came from the rear of the building, 'Stop, whoever's there!'

Suddenly panic-stricken, Hector shoved the file back and closed the cabinet. Tommy ran to the door leading to the hallway and turned the key in the lock. He re-opened the front window and helped Hector to scramble out then followed him. He shut the window and they ran along Argyle Street towards South Street where Hector's Bullnose was parked. Out of breath and wheezing badly as he ran through the West Port, the ancient stone gateway to the town, Hector collided with a man coming the other way. 'Watch out!' the man said in a strong English accent. 'Sorry,' Hector muttered as he rushed on.

Tommy was already in the passenger seat by the time Hector reached his car. It started at the first touch of the button. As they drove along South Street, Sergeant McNeill nowhere in sight, Hector realized the man he had bumped into was Sidney Roper.

'Did you find what you were looking for, sir?' Tommy asked.

'I think I may have,' Hector replied. 'A lot of men in this town had cause to hate Mr Macmillan.'

'You took a hell of a chance, doing that, sir. Jake's lucky to have you.'

'Well I couldn't have done it without you. I'm most grateful. And Jake will be too when he finds out.'

'Aye.' His tone of voice was more expressive than what he said.

After dropping Tommy at his house in Bridge Street, Hector drove home sedately, congratulating himself on a successful mission and relieved it was over. He had never felt more in need of a cigarette. As stealthily as the housebreaker he now was, he let himself in and went into the drawing room. He poured himself a generous dram from the crystal decanter that had been his father's, found the cigarettes and lit up, promising himself that this really would be his last.

Comfortable in his favourite chair, and having noted down all the names and details he could remember, he tried to think through what he had learned. B. Maxwell was almost certainly Brian Maxwell, a fine American golfer who was in town as a competitor in the Amateur Championship. Hector knew him by reputation only. He was rumoured to be exceptionally rich. Hector didn't know whether the crash had changed that. Some years earlier, he had been put up for membership of the Royal and Ancient but had made himself unpopular by writing a newspaper article in which he criticised the Old Course as being hopelessly out of date and in urgent need of substantial changes. If that was not enough, the Club received two scathing letters from American members who knew him. His proposer and seconder had wisely withdrawn his application. The correspondence he had seen did not worry Hector unduly; if Maxwell had formed some grandiose scheme for taking over the St Andrews Links, it was bound to fail as an Act of Parliament would be required to change the present situation. And anyway, it was not Maxwell but the Enright Bank that had leverage over the town and many of its citizens.

Renewing his promise that this would be his last, Hector lit another cigarette, refreshed his glass and turned his mind to Jake. He knew that the surest way of saving him was to find out who had murdered Macmillan and Corbett, and prove it. Tommy was right; he had taken one hell of a chance breaking into the office. Had it been partly guilt that made him do it? Whatever his good intentions, had he failed as a stepfather? It had been on the fifteenth anniversary of Jake's father's death that he had got drunk and expelled. That could be no coincidence. And until he had been arrested he had sometimes been downright disrespectful. Hector had wanted to take a stick to him more than once. John Taylor-Smith, Lavender's first husband and his own best friend, had always been the more daring, Hector the more hidebound by what was right. By breaking in to Macmillan's office, was he subconsciously imitating the fallen hero who cast such a long shadow over the family? He flicked his battle-scarred lighter, which John's mother had handed on to him after his death, and gazed into the flame before lifting his thumb and letting it die. 'Damn you, John,' he muttered. 'Damn you, damn you, damn you.'

He was relieved to find Lavender sleeping soundly when he crept into the bedroom. As he undressed he felt for his handkerchief. He could not find it. He checked again. It was missing. He had been so concerned with placating Lavender that he had forgotten gloves. Had he dropped the handkerchief in Macmillan's office? Was it one of the ones with his initials embroidered on it? He could not remember. Despite the dim lighting, might McNeill have identified his car in South Street as he rushed to Argyle Street? He was a bumbling fool, but even so … And might Roper have recognized him? He didn't think he would have but … As he lay sleepless beside his wife, trying not to wheeze or breathe smoke and whisky over her, fear gripped his stomach.

9

After a few hours Hector was up again, taking the girls back to school with instructions not to talk about Jake's problems. After half term, school had resumed on the previous day but the girls had been kept at home. Discussing matters on Wednesday evening, Hector had insisted to Lavender that it would be best for them to resume their normal lives sooner rather than later and she had reluctantly agreed. Hotchkiss had reported that Jake's appearance before Fairweather had gone as expected and that he would spend the next week on remand in Perth Prison. Horrified, Lavender had insisted that Hector should drive her there to visit him and check on his welfare. He tried unsuccessfully to reassure her that the prison authorities would be careful to make appropriate arrangements for an inmate who was both untried and under eighteen.

When he returned from dropping the girls at school, Lavender was distraught. Hotchkiss had telephoned; Jake had been assaulted the previous evening. It appeared that he had not been seriously injured but had been badly shaken. He was now in solitary confinement for his own safety. Hotchkiss was adamant that Lavender and, in particular the sheriff, should not attempt to visit him as Hector's position had been the reason for the attack. Hotchkiss would go to Perth that morning to check up and would telephone as soon as he returned.

'The best way to help Jake is to find out who is the real murderer,' Hector told Lavender. 'I think we should re-visit Jane Corbett, try to persuade her that Jake is innocent, and see if she can tell us anything.'

As he drove out to Corbett's farm, Hector had never seen Lavender so desolate. Even after John had been killed there had been a spark of determination. Now she seemed resigned to whatever fate had in store. He did not know what to say to lift her and the silence in the car was oppressive. He parked beside the farmhouse, helped her out and rang the bell.

The sheepdog's barking became more ferocious as the door was opened a crack. 'What do you want?' Jane Corbett asked, making no move to quieten the animal.

Hector replied firmly, 'The same as you, Jane. Justice. Please let us in. We need to talk about this.'

'They say your boy killed my husband. Why should I help you?'

'Because it seems Jake is being blamed for someone else's crime. You want Alan's killer to face justice and so do I, even if it does turn out to be Jake.'

He felt Lavender stiffen at this, but it had the desired effect on Jane. The dog was roped and shut away and she opened the door for them. 'Come into the kitchen,' she said. 'The boys have their train set in the sitting room. It takes their minds off …' Her voice caught.

She gestured towards the sturdy wooden chairs round the table and sat down. There was no offer of tea or anything else. She looked expectantly at Hector.

'I believe a lot of people round here were not unhappy to hear about Gordon Macmillan's death,' he began. Her left shoulder twitched in a half-shrug. 'How do you think Alan felt?'

'He didn't say.'

'Did he ever say anything to you about financial problems?'

She scowled. 'How do you know about that?'

'So he did?'

'That's no business of yours.'

'Jane, I can't tell you how I know this, but a lot of people took Gordon Macmillan's financial advice and regretted it. I know that Alan was one of them.' He let that sink in. More softly he added, 'Did he have life insurance?'

She shook her head, her eyes moist. She gulped then said, 'He was very worried. I could tell. But he never said why. He just kept telling me to watch the pennies. Then he got rid of one of the men, said he didn't need him, but he did. He tried to do the work himself but he couldn't. And he took part in that blasted play. Couldn't let people down, he said. Had to keep up appearances.'

'Were you aware of pressure being put on him?'

'What sort of pressure?'

'Anything, strangers visiting, letters?'

'No. Well, there was that letter with the funny writing. It seemed to make him angry but he wouldn't say why.'

'When did it arrive? Was it posted?'

'Yes, it was posted. It arrived last week.'

'May I see it?' Jane's face twitched and she looked searchingly at him. 'It may be a clue as to who killed him.'

He thought she was going to refuse but slowly she got up and left the room, returning with the sheet of cheap paper Hector had seen previously. She handed it to him and Lavender leaned over to examine it too.

'Do you have a mirror, darling?' he asked.

Lavender produced one from her handbag. Hector held it to the right of the page. 'Eureka!' he exclaimed. Reading aloud from the reflection, he continued, '"The Links must be sold.

Vote for that and your debts will be forgiven. Deliver yourself from bankruptcy." It's not signed. I recognised mirror writing from the War. Sometimes it was used to get past the censors. You start on the right side of the page and make the letters backwards so it looks normal in a mirror. They say Leonardo da Vinci used it for stuff he didn't want others to read.' He paused. 'So someone was putting pressure on Alan.'

'What does it mean, "The courses must be sold"?' Lavender asked.

'I have an idea,' Hector said quietly, 'and I don't like it.' Turning to Jane, he asked, 'Can you shed any light on this?'

Miserably, she shook her head. 'Are we nearly bankrupt? Do we have no money?'

Hector didn't know how to respond. 'You need good advice, my dear. That's all I can say.' She dissolved into tears. He got up and put his arm round her heaving shoulders, exchanging despairing looks with Lavender. 'Is there not someone who can help you through this?'

She sniffed. 'Martin, Alan's brother was here yesterday and he said he'd call later today.'

'Good.' He waited until Jane had collected herself. 'May I keep this?' he asked, holding the letter.

She was beyond resisting. Hector folded it and put it in his inside pocket. 'You don't by any chance still have the envelope?' he asked.

She shook her head. 'But I remember it. When Alan got the letter he looked puzzled then went off to the bedroom. He would have recognized mirror writing from the War, I suppose. It was such an odd reaction that I looked at the envelope. It was cheap, like the paper. The writing was in block capitals, with a St Andrews post-mark. It had been posted the day before.'

'Can you remember the day it arrived?'

She looked out of the window, as if for inspiration. 'It was Friday, yes, definitely Friday. We have fish for lunch on Fridays and Alan was still in the bedroom when the fishmonger's boy called. As I say, when he came out of the bedroom he was cross. I could tell, but he just stomped off to check the cattle.'

Hector asked, 'Can you remember any of those at the dinner on Sunday night? It was for those who had played in an Amateur Championship in the past.'

Jane looked puzzled then said, 'Yes, I see why you're asking that. They called themselves a silly name, "The Pams" or something like that. There was Jim Liddell, Clive Laughton, Dennis Bowers, Tom Loveman, Freddie Torkington, and Alan of course. He was quite excited about it and talked about it beforehand. There would have been others, but that's all I can remember.'

'One more thing. Have you ever heard of something called The Andrean Project?'

She appeared genuinely puzzled. 'No. What is it?'

'I'm not sure yet, but it may be connected with Alan's murder.'

She stared at the scuffed linoleum floor and said deliberately, steel in her voice, 'I hope it wasn't your boy, but most of all I want the killer to hang.'

'So do we,' Lavender assured her.

There was no more to be learned from Jane. Thanking her for her help, they hugged her as they left and were glad to feel her respond with a weak squeeze.

*   *   *

Obviously distressed, Mrs Alves greeted them as soon as the wheels of the Bullnose crushed the Ballochmyle gravel: Hector was to telephone Mr Hotchkiss as soon as possible. His heart in his mouth, Hector ran to the phone and after what seemed an interminable wait was put through to Hotchkiss. Calmly, the lawyer described Jake's injuries: a black eye, bruised and possibly cracked ribs and bruised testicles; the boy was scared and unhappy but resigned to a week's solitary confinement; he continued to assert his innocence and had refused to identify his attackers.

'He's learning,' Hector said grimly. He thanked Hotchkiss before reassuring Lavender and Mrs Alves, who had listened intently to what they could hear of the conversation.

'Right,' Hector said to Lavender, 'we need to talk and think. Sherry will help.'

Lavender looked at her watch. It was barely half past eleven. 'Isn't it a bit early?'

'No.'

Smiling at his assertive tone, she went to the drawer where she had put his cigarettes and lighter. 'I see the mice have eaten a couple,' she said as she placed them beside him. 'Come on, you can give up once you've sorted out this mess. Till you do, I want you in top form.'

A smooth Amontillado and a cigarette made him feel much better. 'You know, I think we're making headway,' he told her, and described what he had found in Macmillan's office. He did not mention the handkerchief, McNeill's intervention or Roper.

'What are you doing?' Lavender asked as he picked up the newspaper and turned to the sport pages.

'I'm checking ... ah, yes! Brian Maxwell was beaten

yesterday morning. Six and four,' he added with satisfaction. 'Not as bad as poor Laurence Fishburne, my first round opponent. He lost seven and six in the second round. Maybe I was better out of it.' Noticing her impatient look, he turned to the notes he had taken of Macmillan's files, ticking some names as he went through them. 'I think he's trying to take over the golf courses,' he said. 'He's got a bee in his bonnet about changing and modernising the Old Course, which would be appalling. Listen to this: I've noted ten names, all I could remember last night. Seven of them are town councillors, including Alan Corbett. There's Freddie Torkington ...'

'Freddie? I'd have thought he had more sense. He has such a ghastly wife, Fiona. I wouldn't mind seeing her taken down a peg or two.'

'And there's Clive Matthews, he and Freddie are on the Joint Green Committee. Jim Liddell and Dennis Bowers are both town councillors and were at that dinner on Sunday night. Liddell and his wife were at the after-play party. Another one in financial trouble is Courtney Haversham, the MP. They are all seriously in debt as a result of the stock market crash. And so is the town itself. Now if the council voted to try to sell the courses, and the Joint Green Committee did too, and the local MP was in favour, it would be quite possible to push through the Act of Parliament necessary to enable that to happen.'

'And this Brian Maxwell wants to buy the courses, change the Old Course and get his revenge on the R and A for not giving him membership?'

'That must be it.'

'But why kill Macmillan and Corbett?'

'I don't know yet. I expect Macmillan was killed by someone who had been ruined by his advice. I suppose his killer might have been strongly against the take-over of the golf courses.

Corbett was almost certainly killed to prevent him telling the police what he had seen. I need to find out who was ruined by Macmillan, at the dinner on Sunday night and at the after-play party on Tuesday. So far, apart from poor Alan there is just Freddie Torkington and Jim Liddell. I think I'll head off down to the Club to see if I can learn some more.'

'How can you just sail off to watch golf when Jake's languishing in jail?' Suddenly angry, Lavender's voice rose.

'It's the best way to see people; everyone interested in golf will be there. And I want to put on a good face. Skulking at home would be taken as acceptance of Jake's guilt.'

She shrugged. 'Mrs Alves won't be very pleased. I know she's gone to a lot of trouble over lunch today.'

'Well apologise for me.'

'At least pour me another sherry before you go. I hope you find out something useful.'

*   *   *

The Club was buzzing with talk about the match between Bobby Jones and Harrison Johnston, known as Jimmie, the United States Amateur Champion. Both men had got past their morning opponents and were due to meet after lunch. Hector saw Freddie Torkington in a chair beside the window of the Big Room, face flushed, his tiny chin wobbling as another gin and tonic was dealt with. Hector wondered briefly how the inside of his peculiar neck was configured when Freddie got up and headed for the House of Lords, as the washroom was called.

Hector excused himself from the men he was with and followed Torkington into the spacious room, floored in white marble and boasting unconventional scales with a seat upholstered in red velvet. The cubicles were unoccupied. Hector stood at a

urinal two along from Torkington and next to an elderly member who took a long time to finish his pee. Eventually he shuffled off to wash his hands. As Torkington buttoned up his flies,
Hector heard the old man's deep breathing on his way to the
door and they were alone.

'I say, Freddie,' Hector began, doing up his own buttons,
'did you get an odd sort of letter recently?'

Torkington's shoulders twitched but he managed to say 'No'
as if he hadn't a care in the world.

Hector knew better. 'Not one with funny writing?'

Torkington barged past him and made for a basin where he
washed his hands vigorously. Hector stood watching. Suddenly
Torkington swivelled round and stuck his face close to Hector's.
'Are you behind this?' he hissed.

'No.' Hector looked him in the eye.

Torkington clenched and unclenched his fists. Then he
raised his eyebrows. 'Oh, you must have got one too.'

Thinking quickly, Hector shrugged and nodded.

'Why you?'

'I suppose in case someone tried to interdict them or something arose in court.'

A rueful grin spread across Torkington's face. 'Yes, I see.'
Slowly, he dried his hands. 'You know, I don't think it'll be too
bad once all the dust has settled. We'll still get our golf and
it'll all be a bit more, well, selective, don't you know? But that
bounder, Macmillan. I wish I'd never listened to him. He was
behind these letters, you can be sure of it. I challenged him but
he denied all knowledge. He was a right twister, like all lawyers.
Oh, sorry old man.'

'I agree about Macmillan. Are you going to do what the letter says?'

'No option, have I?' His chin wobbled unhappily.

'Have you spoken to anyone else who …' The door opened and two younger members, obviously well refreshed, burst in.

'Ah, Sheriff, do you think Jones deliberately aimed for the crowd at the seventeenth yesterday?' one asked.

'Absolutely not,' Hector replied. 'He tried to get the people to move back but they wouldn't. Aiming at the crowd is something he just wouldn't do.'

He did not listen to the reply as Torkington had slipped out. Hector followed him but he had joined other company.

During lunch Hector tried not to be preoccupied and found himself defending Jones once more. He was astonished that anyone who knew Jones' record of exemplary sportsmanship should genuinely think that he might deliberately aim at the crowd. He became quite heated in putting down a London stockbroker with a superior manner and had to check himself before he went too far.

10

To Mrs Alves' chagrin, Lavender picked at her lamb chops. Marie and Charlotte were at school and she was alone with her worries. She wished Hector was not so preoccupied with the threat to his golf course and had a feeling that the murderer or murderers might be found nearer home. Macmillan had not been a nice man and Jake had commented how hard he was on Sorley. Had a worm turned? There was one way to find out.

As she leaned her bicycle against the Macmillans' wall, Willie Moncur came out of their gate. They greeted each other in a friendly way and Willie was going on to his own house when Lavender called him. 'May I have a quick word?' she asked.

Willie appeared hesitant, but he walked a few steps back to Lavender.

'How are they?' she asked, noting that a yew hedge prevented them from being seen from the house.

He shuffled from one foot to the other. 'It's difficult for them,' he replied. 'Doris suggested I should give them some shepherd's pie. We had it for lunch and our cook had made more than we needed. I saw Lucy but she and Sorley barely speak. You'll find it awkward, perhaps.'

'What's wrong between them?'

'Sorley had lied to her about being out on Sunday night. He told the truth to the police, that he had been with your boy

Jake when Gordon found them and there had been a row. Now she doubts ...'

'Whether he killed his father?'

Willie nodded unhappily. 'They didn't get on, Sorley and Gordon.' His body tense, he looked up as if for guidance then said, 'Gordon was a stern father, insisting that Sorley should be the best at anything Gordon thought was important. If Gordon didn't think something was important it didn't count. Sorley was a good actor at school but Gordon refused to go to the plays. Lucy wanted to go, she told Doris, but Gordon wouldn't let her. And if Sorley came home with a bad report ... the thrashings, next door we could hear the boy screaming for mercy. And when he was expelled from Glenalmond ... It wasn't nice ...' he shuddered.

Lavender put a hand on his arm. She remembered what she had heard about Willie's childhood. The regime next door had clearly brought back unpleasant memories, but she was in no mood for delicacy. 'You mean he beat him?' she asked.

He looked at her strangely. 'We heard the blows. A window was open. But Sorley made no sound that we could hear. He must have ...'

'What?'

'Well, hated his father. But I'm sure he didn't kill him,' he added quickly.

'What do you remember about Sunday night?' she asked gently.

'Our usual. We listened to *The Sunday Night Epilogue*. Doris read for a bit. Our sitting room is at the back of the house and we weren't aware of any comings and goings next door.' Lavender thought there was a rehearsed quality about this, different from the spontaneous expressions of sympathy for the unhappy boy next door.

'Well I'll see how Lucy is. How's Doris?'

'Working away. You know her.' With a rueful smile he opened his own gate and went in.

As she walked up the narrow path between neat spring borders, the flowers now past, Lavender still had no clear idea about how she should approach Lucy. A maid answered the door and showed her into the drawing room where Lucy sat, dressed in black, clutching a lace handkerchief.

There was nothing fancy about this room; cream-coloured walls were hung with gloomy oil portraits of grim-looking men and one woman. Above the black marble fireplace was a Highland view on a rainy day, bleak, sombre and unwelcoming. She had been in it before but now she was aware how much it was the dead man's room, not Lucy's.

'Hello, Lavender.' Lucy's voice was cold, unlike on her previous visit.

'These are difficult times, Lucy. Do you mind if I sit down?'

Lucy inclined her head towards an upright chair opposite her, facing the afternoon sun. 'What can I do for you?'

'Your husband is dead and my son is accused of his murder. He is innocent, I'm sure. I need to find the truth.'

'What truth do you want to find? That my son killed his own father?'

'If that is the truth, yes. I want the truth whatever it is.'

'Even if the police have got it right and it was Jake?' Noting Lavender's face twitch she added, 'No, I thought not.'

'I'd like to speak to Sorley, please.' Lavender felt herself on the verge of tears; she had to control herself.

'I can't see why not.' Lucy rang for the maid and asked her to tell Master Sorley that Mrs Drummond wanted to have a word with him.

The two women sat in awkward silence until Sorley joined

them. Tall and thin, his handsome face spoiled by acne, with dark hair that flopped into his eyes, Sorley looked apprehensively from one to the other. He didn't sit down.

'I know what you told the police, Sorley,' Lavender said. 'Now Jake's in prison, facing two murder charges. If you know anything that might help him, please tell me.' Her voice caught.

The boy looked at the carpet then faced her, his eyes blazing. 'I told the police the truth. I ran away as soon as Papa started hitting Jake with his crook. I didn't recognise anyone in the *haar*. There were some men who'd been putting on the Himalayas. I heard them heading off towards the New Club. They were quite loud and sounded as if they were drunk. I don't know any more. It was Jake's fault I got expelled from Glenalmond, but you said I'd led him on. I hadn't. Really. He stole the sherry and that evening he went on and on about it being fifteen years since his real father had been killed. I just listened and had some of the sherry. Now you'll be trying to make out that I killed my father. Well, I didn't. I just didn't.' Tears in his eyes, he rushed out of the room. There was the sound of feet running up a wooden staircase.

Lucy looked steadily at Lavender. 'I hope you're satisfied. I know my husband was not popular, and he could be harsh. But he had principles. Iron principles. People don't seem to appreciate that. Now I think you'd better go.'

Feeling that there was more to be learned from that household but reluctantly impressed by the dignity with which the new widow defended her husband, Lavender thanked her and left.

* * *

Out on the course and following the Jones/Johnston match, Hector's mind kept turning over the facts that had emerged. Macmillan was the most likely letter-writer, as he knew who was in debt, and by how much. He had apparently dissociated himself from Maxwell, but that could be just a cover. And yet there was something that jarred.

The match was proving to be something of an anti-climax. Jones was out in level par and one up, then birdied the tenth. By the time he stood on the fourteenth tee he was four up with five to play.

'Johnston hasnae a prayer. I'm aff tae see a real match,' a man wearing a tweed cap whom Hector did not know told him. Hector smiled and nodded. But for his friendship with Jones he might have gone too. Johnston didn't have a prayer and the gallery was shrinking. A prayer, that was it! In the Church of Scotland, the Lord's Prayer asked: 'Forgive us our debts as we forgive our debtors'. In the Anglican Church it was: 'Forgive us our trespasses as we forgive those who trespass against us'. Corbett's letter promised: 'Your debts will be forgiven', and with a clear echo of the Lord's Prayer, went on: 'Deliver yourself from bankruptcy'. Macmillan had been an Anglican and would have been unlikely to phrase the letter that way. Or might that be another smokescreen? Had Maxwell written the letters himself, or had he another accomplice?

Walking deep in thought down the flat part of the fourteenth fairway known as the Elysian Fields, Hector felt a nudge on his elbow. It was O.B. Keeler. 'Bearing up, Hector?' he asked. 'I've heard about your troubles. Eleanor's terribly worried. Would Lavender like her to call? Sometimes at difficult times it's best to leave folks alone. We haven't known what to do. Bob and Mary are concerned for you, too.'

'I'm fine, O.B. thank you,' Hector lied. 'But there is one

thing you might be able to help me with. What do you know about Brian Maxwell?'

'He's a horse's ass. He had a messy divorce from some society dame a few years back and settled out of court so his affairs weren't put under the spotlight. Why?'

'This sounds crazy, but I think he may be trying to buy up the golf course. Macmillan was mixed up in the business and Alan Corbett was involved too.'

'Buy the golf course? You can't mean this one?' O.B. snorted derisively. A man walking in front of them turned sharply.

'Yes, and if he did, he'd make all sorts of alterations to the Old Course,' Hector whispered and led O.B. aside. 'A lot of people here, through Macmillan, invested in U.S. stocks and have come badly unstuck. Those who have any say in running the Links are being pressurised to sell.'

O.B. screwed up his face. 'You mean this, don't you? It's crazy, but Maxwell would be just the S.O.B. to do it, if it could be done. He's mighty proud of his Scots ancestry. His enemies call him "MacSwell".'

'Did he not get hit by the crash?'

'I believe not. He made a fortune out of bootlegging and his business continued to do well when honest men have gone to the wall. Then he took an interest in the stock market and I've heard he was one of the worst short-sellers, making a packet out of everyone else's misfortune.'

'I don't know much about stocks and shares,' Hector confessed. 'My stockbroker in Edinburgh tells me what to put my money into, generally as a result of a tip he's got at Muirfield, and I take his advice. What's short-selling?'

'If you think a share is over-valued and due to fall, a so-called bubble, you sell it at the current price, even though you don't own it, on the basis that you'll buy it back some time in the future at whatever price it then has. If you're right and it falls, you make money, but if it rises you lose. Big time. Something to do with margins, I believe. Short-sellers made a pile of dollars during the crash. This year there was a brief recovery, but that has turned out to be what they call a "dead cat bounce" and it's going down again. The short-sellers are making another fortune. There was an American financier in the last century, Daniel Drew, who explained short-selling: "He who sells what isn't his'n, must buy it back or go to pris'n". That's about it.'

'I think I see,' Hector said doubtfully. 'Do you know anything about the Enright Bank of Connecticut?'

'Not much. I do know a lot of banks are going under. I have a broker friend in New York. I can ask him, and I'll also inquire about Maxwell.'

'Thank you, O.B. That would be most helpful. While you're at it, ask about a broker called Harvey Feinstein. He seems to be mixed up in it as well. And Lavender would appreciate a call from Eleanor, I'm sure. Look, they're at the green already. Bob's probably won by now.'

'Jimmie Johnston's a terrier. He never gives up. The St Andrews motto, *dum spiro spero*, while I breathe I hope, could have been written for him. But no one can give Bob a lead of four up with five to play and win.'

By the time they caught up, the players were making their way to the fifteenth tee. Johnston had won the fourteenth with a birdie four. Jones made a mess of the fifteenth and they halved the sixteenth. Hector saw that O.B. was becoming increasingly nervous. When Johnston won the seventeenth with a fine birdie four, O.B. whispered, his voice shaking, 'In the Western Amateur Championship, Jimmie was once five down with six to play and won by one hole.'

'He wasn't playing Bob,' Hector replied, but he too realized how demoralising it was when an apparently unassailable lead was whittled away. Jones required a half on the final hole to win, but after what had happened, the momentum was with Johnston. If they went down the nineteenth, Hector could not see Jones winning.

Neither golfer played a good second to the eighteenth and both were a long way beyond the pin. Johnston's approach putt was better than Jones'. Facing a downhill, curly eight-footer for a four and for the match, Jones stroked his ball into the centre of the cup. He had survived another tough afternoon by the skin of his teeth.

'I'll book a telephone call to my friend in New York this evening,' O.B. promised as he said goodbye to Hector, adding, 'And Eleanor will be sure to call Lavender.'

In the Club, Hector found Jim Liddell, not his favourite person, in the crowded Big Room, discussing the match with someone he didn't know. As casually as he could, he joined them. Liddell carried on with what he was saying as if Hector wasn't there then turned to him.

'Oh hello, Hector. I'm surprised to see you here.'

Momentarily taken aback, Hector stammered, 'It was a jolly good match.' The man to whom Liddell had been talking slipped away into the throng. 'I hope I'm not interrupting?'

'Not at all, my dear chap. Not at all.' The supercilious grin on Liddell's face made Hector want to punch him. At his peak as a golfer at the same time as Freddie Torkington, Liddell had been the more successful player, and the less popular. Though never actually caught cheating, there were those who swore that the 'leather mashie' was the best club in his bag, as he always seemed to find a good lie in the rough. He attributed his remarkable recovery shots to his long, powerful arms, but

there was a lingering doubt that a nudge with his foot sometimes helped. Short of stature but wiry, with thick, dark hair
and a round, brown face prematurely wrinkled, Hector thought
he resembled an elderly chimpanzee.

Hector decided he should be direct. 'I gather you were in
the group that went putting on the Himalayas on Sunday night?'

Liddell nodded.

'I wonder, did you see anything unusual before you came
in? I understand the *haar* put an end to it.'

'I could only make out shapes. I did hear Macmillan shouting, at least I assume it was Macmillan. "Degenerates" was a
word I picked up.'

'Did you just go back to the New Club?'

'Is this an interrogation?'

'My son has been accused of murder, and I believe him to
be innocent. I have to find out as much as I can about what else
was happening nearby at the time.'

'At the time of the killing? Well, I picked up my ball and
went back to the New Club with the rest, and if you ask them, I
assume they'll tell you that's the truth. One person who didn't
make it back was Freddie Torkington. He said something about
needing a pee and we didn't see him again. I thought it odd at
the time; we'd been putting for pennies and he was three pence
up on me. He always likes to collect his winnings, if he's lucky
enough to win, but he hasn't bothered about that threepenny
bit. It's burning a hole in my pocket.' He jingled his change to
emphasise the point. 'Will that be all? I assume I won't need to
contact my solicitor?'

'If you really have nothing to hide,' Hector said, looking
down his nose at Liddell. 'But thank you. Oh, one other thing,'
he added as the elderly chimp turned away, 'I don't suppose
you've received a rum sort of letter in mirror writing?'

'I have no idea what you're talking about,' he replied, but a tic beside his eye gave him away.

'Or you're not going to tell me,' Hector snapped.

'I can understand why you're desperate.' Giving him a patronizing smile, Liddell moved away.

Anxious to question Torkington about what he had done after the putting, Hector looked round but could not find him. Thinking over what Liddell had said, on his way to his car, Hector saw Tommy. He was limping and the area round his left eye was swollen and red. 'There was a fight in the caddie shed,' he explained. 'Someone said Mr Jones played at the crowd on purpose yesterday and I had to put them right. He's got two of these,' he added grimly, pointing to his injured eye.

'Have you found work this week after our unpleasant Monday?' Hector asked.

'I cannae leave Jeannie for long, sir. I was coming to ask your advice.'

'About what? What's wrong with Jeannie?' Hector knew that Tommy worried about his young sister, whose weak chest had been a frequent cause of concern.

'It's her chest, sir, as usual. Dr Sheach says she'll have to go to a sanatorium. You know, one of these places for poor folk with TB. I've heard they're like prisons. That would kill her, sir, I know it.'

Dr Sheach was reputed to be the town's least effective doctor. Hector often said he'd rather go to a good vet than accept treatment from him and he had heard nothing good about the sanatoria for the poor.

'Would you like Dr Moncur to have a look at her?' he asked. 'Some say she's the best doctor in town, even if she's a woman.'

'Anything that might help, sir. Thank you.'

It was a short walk to the Moncurs' house in Windmill

Road. Doris herself answered the door dressed in trousers and a sweater and invited them in. As it was a professional rather than a social call she showed them to the room she used as a surgery. The wooden floor needed a polish, the red rug which covered the middle of the room was threadbare, the windows were dirty and the furniture worn. A bookcase held a large number of what looked like textbooks from the previous century. At waist height was a shelf containing books that seemed well-used but newer. On the large desk stood a contraption with a rubber airbag Hector guessed was for taking blood pressure. After explaining why they had come and promising to pay her fee, Hector paid close attention as the doctor questioned Tommy.

He had his own reasons for doing so; Dr Henry McNaughton, who had helped him through his recuperation from mustard gas, was about to retire. While he wanted to go to Dr White, a young man and a good golfer who had come to St Andrews recently, Lavender favoured Doris Moncur. As she said, Doris was reputed to be the best doctor in the town. Although she had spent two years assisting in McNaughton's practice, Hector had an inbuilt uneasiness about consulting a woman; after all, what if he had piles? But her questioning of Tommy showed skill and sensitivity. She soon established that, though Jeannie could hardly breathe, there was no blood in the sputum, which she brought up sparingly, she did not have night sweats and was not feverish. There had been no noticeable weight loss and Tommy and his mother were both fine. Producing a pristine-looking stethoscope, she told Tommy to roll up his shirt so that she might listen to his chest. As he did so, Hector saw further evidence of the battle in the caddie shed.

'Right,' she said and allowed herself a crooked smile, which lit up her face. For a moment Hector thought she looked attractive. If she took more care over her appearance and dress and lost a bit of weight she would be a handsome woman, he thought.

She got up and left the room, returning with a jar of dry mustard and a bag of flour, which she placed in her medical bag. Then she led them out to the driveway where a four-door Speed Six Bentley sat. It had been the talk of the town three months earlier when Doris and her brother returned from a trip to the United States and the Bentley was delivered soon afterwards. Apparently Willie had played some big money-matches and won. The car represented his winnings topped up by his grateful backers.

Hector sat in the front passenger seat. Prompted by Tommy in the back, who could not keep the excitement out of his voice, Doris told them with pride that it was this model that Woolf Barnato had driven from Cannes to Calais and then on to London, arriving before the Blue Train, which had set off at the same time, reached Calais.

'Wasn't Dale Bourne, the golfer, with him?' Hector asked.

'I believe so,' Doris replied as they drew up outside Tommy's house in Bridge Street.

The unexpected arrival of a different doctor and the sheriff threw Tommy's mother into confusion, curtseying and calling Hector 'my lord'. While Hector tried unsuccessfully to put her at ease, Doris went to the bedroom to examine her patient.

Five minutes later she emerged with good news; she did not believe Jeannie had tuberculosis and a sanatorium would do her no good. The problem was that she was unable to bring up the sputum, which was congesting her lungs. Doris asked for a clean dishcloth and some warm water. When Tommy brought them she made a paste of the flour and mustard and spread it over the cloth. She then folded the cloth and returned to

the bedroom. 'There's nothing like some old-fashioned reme-
dies,' she said. 'Mustard poultices are excellent for stimulat-
ing a cough. The more sputum she brings up the better.' With
instructions to remove it after twenty minutes and apply three
times a day, she and Hector left. She did not take the flour and
mustard with her. 'Contact me at any time if she deteriorates,'
was her final order. Back in the Bentley, she refused to accept
any payment. 'Unlike a lot of people, you have always supported
my brother. I'm delighted to help your caddie's sister,' she said,
her jaw set, her eye on the road ahead. 'I heard the news about
your son. I'm sorry,' she added.

'Thank you,' Hector said.

'I suppose you will have a good counsel for him?'

'MacGregor Mitchell KC, is the unofficial leader of the Scottish criminal bar. There's a distant family connection, so I hope
we'll get him.'

She smiled. 'I'm very pleased to hear it.'

Dropped off beside his own comparatively modest car, Hector was persuaded that Doris should be their next doctor.

Back at Ballochmyle, he and Lavender were comparing
notes when the doorbell rang. Mrs Alves answered it and came
in to say that PC Gemmell wished to see the sheriff, 'but he's
not in uniform,' she added.

Leaving his whisky in the sitting room, Hector went to the
drawing room to see his unexpected guest. Gemmell came in,
his manner awkward. Hector assumed he had come to apologise for their row after Jake's arrest and was surprised when,
without being asked, the young policeman sat on a hard chair
facing him.

'You know I've always respected you, Sheriff,' Gemmell
began.

Hector smiled acknowledgement.

'I just wondered if you might have lost this.' He produced from his jacket pocket a folded piece of white linen.

Aware that his face had given him away, 'I don't think so,' Hector spluttered.

Gemmell held it up. 'See, Sheriff, it has H.N.D. embroidered. Do you know anyone else with these initials?'

'Not off-hand, no.'

'I found it in the strangest place ...' he paused.

Apprehension gave way to anger; the whippersnapper was playing him like a salmon. The gauche boy-policeman had grown up. Hector glared but said nothing.

Gemmell looked him in the eye. 'I found it when we were investigating a break-in at Mr Macmillan's office. Last night.'

'Really?'

'Yes. In a file that was most interesting.' He put the handkerchief back in his pocket.

'Indeed?'

'It looks as if someone called Maxwell is trying to buy the golf courses.'

'That would be terrible.'

'I think so, Sheriff, but not against the law, unlike for example, breaking into an office, even an unoccupied office.'

'And have you caught the culprit?'

'No. Sergeant McNeill surprised him but he got away, probably in a rush.'

Hector felt some relief, but he wanted to get to the point. 'Why are you telling me this?'

'I've always respected you, Sheriff, as I said. If Mr Macmillan was trying to help someone to take over our golf courses, it might have been a reason to kill him. And the courses belong to the town. Everyone can play them. That mustn't change. Golf mustn't become something only people with money can enjoy.'

'I quite agree, and it would be particularly serious if the person taking over was intent on fundamentally changing the Old Course.'

'I heard there's going to be an emergency meeting of the Town Council tomorrow morning at ten-thirty. It's about selling the courses. The town's nearly bankrupt, Sheriff.'

Hector stifled his gasp of surprise. Events were moving fast, too fast.

'But I can't see the council voting away our courses. What do you think, Sheriff?' The young policeman searched Hector's face for reassurance he could not give.

Without pausing to go over the pros and cons, Hector decided to take Gemmell into his confidence without actually admitting the break-in. 'This is unofficial, Gemmell, at least for now. But some people on the Town Council and the Joint Green Committee have been put under pressure. They've been sent anonymous letters in a code that was used during the War, telling them to vote for a sale. If they do, the debts they ran up speculating on American stocks will be cancelled. I bet the people behind this are pushing for a vote knowing they are likely to win and before this business becomes common knowledge.'

It was Gemmell's turn to look shocked. 'What can we do?' he whispered.

'Well public opinion is going to be against them and they won't get anywhere without an Act of Parliament. I have reason to think they will try to get the MP, Courtney Haversham, to support them. If we could swing Haversham to go against them, exposing their blackmail tactics, that should put an end to it.'

'Have they tried to blackmail Haversham?'

'I don't know but I suspect they have.'

'Is there anything we can do about the meeting, sir?'

'I wish I could think of something, short of organising some sort of protest which probably wouldn't achieve anything. Councillors would have to choose between solvency and bankruptcy, for themselves and the town. I can't see many voting for bankruptcy.'

Gemmell's disappointment showed in his tone of voice. 'So we just sit back and let it happen, sir?'

'Not at all. Dammit, I have to think, then do something effective. And I bet the two murders are related to this.'

'I have to say I agree with you but I should go, sir,' Gemmell said, rising from his chair.

'Wait. If the murders are related to this, my son is innocent. I can't ask you to go against your superiors, but you probably know that there was an after-dinner putting match on the Himalayas just before Macmillan's murder. The *haar* put a stop to it. It involved a group known as "The Pams". Two of the participants were Freddie Torkington and Jim Liddell. They were both at the after-play party during which Alan Corbett was killed. Torkington is on the Joint Green Committee and Liddell is a town councillor. I have reason to believe that both are seriously in debt to the same American bank. I know that Torkington and Corbett both received coded letters telling them to vote for a sale of the courses. Another thing, while the rest of the putters went back to the New Club, according to Liddell, Torkington said something about needing a pee and didn't appear back at the Club. He told me he remembered shouting from the direction of the second on the Old but didn't mention needing a pee. I don't have the power to question people, as they need to be questioned, and I have a very obvious interest. I wish someone with the authority to make enquiries might do so. I can't say more than that to you. Oh, except that my wife is suspicious of young Sorley Macmillan. His father was cruel to him, I believe, and he had the opportunity to commit both murders.'

During this speech, Gemmell had stood over Hector in silence, listening intently. 'I hear you, Sheriff,' he said then removed the handkerchief from his pocket for a second time. 'I'll just leave this with you. It's not yours, of course, but it has your initials and you might as well get the use of it as we don't know whose it is.' He dropped it into Hector's lap. 'Inspector McTaggart would flay me alive if he got to hear of this, sir.'

'He won't. It would look bad for me too.' He stuffed the handkerchief into a pocket. 'Look, Gemmell, I'm terribly grateful, you know. Really, terribly grateful. And we must keep in touch, but carefully and unofficially. I loathe these accursed telephone things but they have their uses. Remember though that the operator will often be listening in. If we need to talk confidentially there's nothing to beat a face-to-face meeting.'

Once he had seen the young policeman out, Lavender called him. Dinner had been ready for ten minutes, but she was hungrier for information than for food.

*   *   *

'I can't see old Freddie killing people. He's such a nice, companionable man,' Lavender commented over dinner. Hector had recounted his meeting with Gemmell and she had cheered up noticeably.

'You never know what someone's capable of if they're pushed too far, old girl.'

'Well, as Freddie's resisted the temptation to murder Fiona all these years, I can't see him killing Macmillan and Alan Corbett now. What about Liddell?'

'I don't care for him; he's, to use your word for Sorley, sleekit. But he was very assured as he answered my questions. I hope Gemmell checks with the other Pams that he did go back to the Club with the rest. But, despite the fact that I've always regarded him as a good egg, it's Freddie who has questions to answer.'

'Will you try to see him again?'

'I'd rather leave that to Gemmell. I have no authority to quiz people, and Freddie will know that. Gemmell's a good lad. He'll do his best, but ultimately he'll have to do what McTaggart says.' He paused. 'Talking of Freddie, I wonder what the hangman would do if ...' Seeing Lavender's face cloud over, he regretted what he had just said.

Lavender pushed food round her plate then asked, 'How many votes will Maxwell and co need to get this through the council tomorrow?'

'I suppose about a dozen. I wish Norman Boase was still provost. He would kill this stone dead.'

'Yes. Arnott doesn't have anything like his stature. But they'll need more than just the names you got from Macmillan's files. Do you think some will vote for a sale because they really think it's for the best?'

'Possibly a few, but I wouldn't be surprised if Maxwell had some other sort of hold over the ones not in a financial mess. Lawyers know a lot of secrets about people and if Macmillan breached client confidentiality he might have spilled some rather nasty beans. One thing that niggles me is that the money is owed to the Enright Bank, and I don't see how Maxwell could force them to take court proceedings against those who stood up to him. That would be a matter for them and with debt, it's sometimes sensible to go easy on the debtor, play the long game.'

At this point an harassed Mrs Alves bustled in. 'Sorry to interrupt, sir, Mrs Drummond. The telephone rang as I was passing it. It's Mr Keeler for the sheriff. He sounded as if it was urgent.'

Still chewing, Hector got up from the table. He listened to what O.B. had to say then returned to the dining room. 'I'm going to see O.B. now,' he said. 'He's getting some important information from America.'

'What about your dinner, sir?' Mrs Alves wailed as he rushed out of the front door.

11

O.B. was in a state of high excitement when he greeted Hector in the lounge of the Grand Hotel. 'Come up to my room, Hector. I've booked a call from Joe Rubin, my broker friend in New York. It's just after lunchtime there and he was going to see some guys, ask some questions.'

Waving a greeting to Eleanor, who was sitting with Bob and Mary Jones, Hector followed O.B. upstairs. While O.B. perched on the side of the bed next to the telephone, Hector occupied an easy chair with a splendid view over the links. Between the golf courses and the North Sea lay the West Sands, acres of flat beach that were bracing summer and winter. Hector remembered as a child running from the dunes where he had changed, shivering and watching out for dead jellyfish, into the distant, salty chill of the sea. This was all part of his hometown, and he loved everything about it with a visceral intensity.

It was still light and he could see a group finishing their round. Squinting into the setting sun, and cursing the mustard gas that had permanently weakened his sight, he managed to recognise four caddies, able to play the great course as part of their birthright as citizens of St Andrews. That was something precious that had to be preserved. He felt a surge of anger that someone from a distant country should have the nerve to try to take it over and alter the great course according to his whim. If they had committed murder as well, and framed his stepson, he would destroy them, whatever the cost. Turning towards O.B., who was watching him with a look of sympathy and concern, Hector slowed his breathing. 'A grand sight,' he said, trying to keep the emotion out of his voice.

'Worth preserving, Hector.'

'Indeed.'

The silence that followed was broken by the ring of the telephone. O.B. answered and was quickly put through to his broker friend. Hector could not follow the conversation; the broker was doing most of the talking and there were silences between speakers. Hector remembered that the sound waves had to cross the Atlantic in a cable.

'I'll be damned … son of a bitch … wow!' O.B. exclaimed. Hector became increasingly impatient.

At last O.B. put down the receiver.

'Well?' said Hector.

'Joe's a good guy,' O.B. began. 'He's smart but honourable and I trust him. When I spoke to him earlier he confirmed what I told you going down fourteen, that Brian Maxwell is a horse's ass, but bright. He trained as a lawyer but didn't practise. He made his first fortune from bootlegging and hookers and has always managed to keep one step ahead of the law. He uses bribery and blackmail to coax men into his way of thinking. They say he has a team of swell-looking hookers who take time out of their usual schedule to lure over-eager law enforcement guys into extra-marital affairs. Oh, and you should never play cards with him, at least not for money. Last year he was one of the few to see that the stock market would stop rising and he started short-selling. He's made more this year by spotting the "dead cat bounce" for what it is. Harvey Feinstein is out of the same mould and they're buddies. Joe didn't know much about the

Enright Bank, but he promised to ask around when he went out to lunch. He's just told me that, like many small banks, it's in trouble, or was. Maxwell and Feinstein targeted it in April and, by short-selling and buying back more shares rather than taking profit, they own nearly thirty per cent of the bank. Worse, Maxwell has bought up parcels of debt owed to the bank so the debtors will be due to pay him. I think we can guess that he will have bought the debts owed by St Andrews Town Council and men like Corbett. So he will be able to bankrupt them at will.'

'That's serious.'

'And that's not all. After a few Martinis, Maxwell was overheard boasting that he'd let Bobby Jones win the British Amateur but he'd win the golf course, make some big changes to create a fabulous test of golf and found an exclusive club. As he'd got the local planning authorities in his pocket he'd build a great clubhouse and hotel next to the first tee. I guess he means on the Bruce Embankment.'

'That should never be allowed.' The Bruce Embankment was the grassy area lying between the first fairway and the North Sea. An hotel there would block the view of the West Sands and ruin a world-famous site. Hector thought for a moment. Quietly he said, 'You know, he's right. He will have the planning authorities in his pocket. While most towns are having their planning decisions transferred to county councils, St Andrews and Thurso Town Councils are retaining their existing powers.'

'But won't there be an uproar when people hear about all this?'

'Yes, but Maxwell and, presumably, Macmillan have been very clever. There is to be an emergency meeting of the town council at ten-thirty tomorrow morning. Word hasn't got round yet and there won't be time to organise opposition. It will go through, you can be sure of that. However, that's not the end of it. As the governance of the Links is laid down in an Act of Parliament, it will need another Act to authorise the sale. And that's where the MP, Courtney Haversham, comes in.' Hector told O.B. about the people ruined by Macmillan's advice and the anonymous letters in mirror writing. 'The two murder victims were both tied up in this business, and I bet they were murdered because of it. Why, I don't know. Yet. You don't want to know how I learned all this,' he added.

O.B. frowned then shrugged. 'The strange thing is, Maxwell checked out of his room here after he lost yesterday, but the rosy-cheeked lady at reception told me he's due back later tomorrow. He has a reservation for dinner,' O.B. said.

'That'll be Mary. She's a very nice lady. Talks the hind legs off a donkey and loves a gossip.'

'Well she sure has the knack of making person-to-person calls across the Atlantic. I'll have to leave her a nice tip when I go.'

'I really appreciate your help in this, O.B. These calls are expensive, I know.'

'Hector, I'm a journalist, and the only story bigger than this would be if Bob won the Amateur and Open Championships on both sides of the Atlantic in a single year. I'll write a book about this one day, and I'll send you a copy.'

'I think on my way out I'll have a chat with Mary, the receptionist I mean. Will you be in the lounge?'

'Yes. Eleanor believes I'm up to something, but I haven't told her or Bob. This would make him mad as hell and I don't want to upset him. These eighteen-hole matches make him nervous enough without some S. O. B. trying to buy the golf course from under him then spoil it.'

Normally, Hector would have stopped to chat in the lounge

but he saw a guest leaving Mary alone in reception. 'Hello, Mary,' he said warmly.

'Oh my lord, it's you! What can I do for you, my lord?' She had an exaggerated notion of Hector's importance, which he usually found somewhat irritating. This time he was going to play on it.

'It'll have been a busy week, I bet?' he said.

'Oh yes, my lord.'

'A lot of trans-Atlantic calls, Mr Keeler was saying.'

'Oh yes.'

'Mary, may I take you into my confidence? I'm concerned about the activities of a Mr Maxwell, who was staying here earlier in the week. He may be involved in illegality. Can you tell me anything you may have overheard operating the telephone switchboard?'

Mary looked round to check no one was listening. 'Well my lord, Mr Maxwell is no gentleman. He's been here for the last fortnight. Very rude, ignorant I would say. Never says please or thank-you. That made it surprising.' She paused, as if expecting Hector to know what she was talking about.

'What's surprising?'

'That he is such good friends with Mr Haversham.'

'The MP? Courtney Haversham?'

'Yes my lord. I was surprised that a real gentleman like Mr Haversham should have much time for him. I voted for Mr Haversham last year and in the election before that, my lord. Our betters know best, I always think. I don't hold with socialism, even if Mr MacDonald is a nice man, and Scottish. We may be equal before God, but He has given us all different stations in life and we should accept that. You can be poor and happy, my lord, and I see a lot of rich people coming to this hotel who are anything but happy.'

'I'm sure that's right, and I'm surprised too that Mr Haversham should be friends with Mr Maxwell.' Hector tried to re-direct Mary's flow of information.

'Well my lord,' her voice dropped to a whisper, 'I couldn't help but overhear – I wasn't eavesdropping, my lord,'

'Of course not,' Hector murmured.

'Mr Haversham is going to be Mr Maxwell's guest, at Gleneagles, if you please. They'll probably be there this very minute. After Mr Maxwell lost in the Amateur Championship yesterday morning he was on the telephone to the House of Commons in London. I'd never before put a guest through to there, and they're not very efficient although they're full of airs and graces. It took them ages to find Mr Haversham but they did eventually. Mr Maxwell said something about a project going well but he really wanted to speak to Mr Haversham about the next step. Mr Haversham said he could get away tomorrow, that is this morning. I remember his very words: "The Iron and Steel Industries bore me to death. Winston Churchill can say what's needed to be said and I'd prefer to sleep in the train than try and stay awake in the House." What do you think of that?' She didn't pause to hear what Hector thought. 'Anyway my lord he should have arrived at Gleneagles about now. With his valet, if you please! Mr Haversham asked particularly if he might bring him. As if they don't have enough staff at Gleneagles! I think they're planning something, my lord. Mr Haversham and Mr Maxwell I mean. Mr Haversham said he'd have the year of Mr Adamson, the Secretary of State for Scotland.'

Hector raised his eyebrows.

Mary continued, 'He said this my lord: "He's a good chap even if he is a Socialist and pretty thick with MacDonald". What do you think he meant by having the year of Mr Adamson?'

'Maybe he said he had the ear of Mr Adamson,' Hector suggested.

'Oh.' She was briefly silenced.

'And Mr Maxwell is due to come back here tomorrow in time for dinner, I believe?'

'Yes my lord. He arranged to play golf on the King's Course with Mr Haversham tomorrow morning.'

'Did Mr Maxwell have contact with anyone, particularly locals, while he was staying here?'

'I can't say he did. He often went out walking after dinner, but I don't know where he went, and he was sometimes quite late coming back. There were letters too, of course.'

'Did they come by post?'

'Yes my lord. The envelopes were mostly typed, as I recall. They looked like business letters. Oh, and Mr Macmillan, the man who died, he visited Mr Maxwell last Saturday.'

'Really, how long did he stay?'

'Not long, my lord. Maybe twenty minutes. He left looking very cross, Mr Macmillan, I mean.'

After Hector had thanked Mary and asked her to keep their conversation confidential, he sought out O.B. 'She thinks I'm a cross between the Lord Justice-General and Wyatt Earp,' he explained. 'I should really put her right but she's been most useful. I don't think there's anything I can do about this meeting tomorrow. I think I'll drive up to Gleneagles and see what I can find out there. If Haversham travels with his valet, I'll take mine.'

'You mean Tommy?'

'Who else? Wish Bob luck against young Eric Fiddian.'

'Thank you. He's good, Fiddian, isn't he?'

'Yes. He has a lovely free action and hits the ball a mile. I don't know how he'll react to playing Bob in front of a big

St Andrews crowd. He's English, not Scottish, so support will be divided.'

*   *   *

'Gleneagles? Now?' Lavender demanded.

'Yes. I have to strike while the iron is hot. I can get there in a couple of hours. Haversham's support is crucial to Maxwell's scheme and if I can derail it I might flush out the murderer or murderers.'

'I? You mean we.'

'Well yes, I do.'

'So what are you going to do when you get there and find Maxwell and Haversham drinking whiskies? What will be your excuse for arriving at a ridiculously late hour?'

'I'm not sure yet. I'll think of something.'

'You'll say that I needed a break and we decided to leave only this evening. Yes, I'm coming. Mrs Alves can look after the girls.'

'I was going to take Tommy as my valet. Haversham's bringing his and Tommy might learn something useful from him.'

'Good idea. But what about his sister?'

'I'm sure after treatment from Doris she'll be on the mend. His mother will cope fine. If he realizes it's important to us he'll help.'

'Well, you go to see him now. I suppose if he's prepared to go housebreaking, pretending to be a valet isn't asking much. I'll pack for myself and lay out your stuff. We'd better give Tommy a quick course in valeting,' she added.

'I hadn't thought …'

'He has to have some idea of what he's supposed to be doing. Don't worry, I'll check there are no holes in your socks or underwear. Are you sure Gleneagles can take us?'

'It's immense. It couldn't possibly be full. All the same I'd better telephone to check.'

As Lavender arranged to leave Mrs Alves in charge of the house and began her packing, Hector spoke to the hotel receptionist. A well-spoken lady, she registered no surprise when he booked a room for his wife and himself for that night only, with accommodation in the servants' wing for his valet.

When he arrived unannounced at Tommy's home he was told that Jeannie seemed better already; she had coughed up 'a lot of muck' after her poultice and was breathing more easily. Hector asked if he might speak with Tommy alone and was shown into his bedroom. Blushing at the pile of unwashed clothes, the unmade bed and the black mould discolouring the walls in one corner, Tommy asked Hector if he wanted to sit down. He lowered himself onto the bed, the hard, lumpy mattress reminding him of school, and brought the lad up to date.

'I don't like to leave Jeannie,' Tommy said, shuffling from one foot to the other, 'but I'll ask my mam.'

Tommy's mother was adamant that he should help the sheriff, who had been so good to them. 'There's Betsy next door if I need her, which I'm sure I won't,' she reassured her son, who remained doubtful. Hector could not tell whether he was more concerned for his sister or apprehensive about going to a posh hotel pretending to be a valet. He suspected his caddie thought helping a gentleman to dress was no job for a real man, a view he held himself.

It did not take Tommy long to get ready. When they arrived at Ballochmyle, the lad wearing his best suit, a shapeless brown tweed, Lavender took him in hand. In Jake's room, ignoring the packet of cigarettes and matches she found at the bottom of his sock drawer, she selected a dark pin-stripe suit, a white shirt with a stiff collar, black socks, shoes and a grey tie. Leaving him to change, she told Hector to wait outside the room. 'He's bound to need help, especially with the collar, and he'll be less embarrassed with you.'

Hector waited for a minute then went to see how the lad was getting on. Not well. Although Tommy was three years older, Jake was the same height but bulkier. The shirt billowed round him and the trousers needed continuous hitching up. When Hector entered he was inspecting the starched collar with the same expression as when assessing a bad lie in the rough.

Hector showed him how the collar studs worked and, awkward with the physical proximity, secured the collar round his caddie's neck, the tie tucked under the fold. He knotted the tie and stood back to assess his handiwork.

'A bit loose but it'll have to do,' he commented. 'Now you'd better undo it. You can't sleep in it, you know. I suppose you'd better try to do it yourself. I won't be able to help you tomorrow morning. ' He chuckled.

Even in front of a mirror, the collar remained stubbornly secure. Eventually, with Hector standing behind him and guiding his fingers, Tommy freed himself from the tie then the collar. Reversing the process was beyond him. Shaking his head, Hector searched in Jake's drawers and found a wing collar.

'You don't have to tuck the tie under the fold with this one. It's generally butlers who wear these things but you'll find this easier.' He used a spare stud to soften the slits and handed the collar to Tommy, who managed with some difficulty. A belt was found to hold up the trousers and a liberal quantity of pomade smoothed down and darkened his ginger curls.

'I'd make quite a good valet, I think,' Hector commented. 'Is there anything further I can do to assist your lordship?'

No hint of a smile cracked Tommy's stony face. He felt

ridiculous and more ill at ease than during the housebreaking expedition.

They went to Hector and Lavender's bedroom. It did not take her long to show Tommy how Hector's leather suitcase should be packed and she gave him an old, scuffed one for his clothes. Lastly, she took him into the bathroom and, ignoring his blushes, scrubbed his hands and filed his nails. 'We'll have to do something about this,' she said, lightly touching his black eye and noticing him wince. She got a small tub out of the cabinet and, with great care, rubbed a small amount of ointment into the bruised skin. Tommy saw and felt the softness of her skin and inhaled her delicate floral perfume. Never before had he smelt anything so feminine. It was a moment he would remember and treasure, but secretly. 'You didn't get this in a fight, remember,' she warned, 'You walked into an open cabinet door.'

Downstairs, Tommy watched as Hector fitted the cases into the boot of his Bullnose and they set off into the last, subdued light of a long summer evening. On the way, Hector and Lavender continued to instruct Tommy about the life and duties of a valet. Coming into Glen Devon, Tommy muttered, 'I'll be glad to get back to being a caddie.'

Lavender turned round to face him. 'Remember, Tommy, we don't know exactly who is dangerous, so be on your guard. Jake is innocent, we're sure of that, and we must learn more about what has been going on. If you can talk to Haversham's valet, he might tell you something important, so try to remember everything, no matter how trivial it may seem. We're terribly grateful to you ...' her voice suddenly caught.

'We are, you know,' Hector said. 'And it's not just Jake's future at stake, but our golf course.'

They drove on in silence until there was a bump under the

car. 'Rabbit,' Hector said, but all three were too preoccupied by their different thoughts to care.

Soon they drove up to the grand entrance of Gleneagles Hotel. Hector wiped his eyes, strained by the night driving and said, 'Right, Thomas, do your duty.' Tommy nipped out of the back and opened Lavender's door with a slight bow.

Taken aback by the scale and grandeur of the splendid hotel, owned and operated by the Caledonian Railway Company, a mere six years old and already world-famous, Tommy felt like a fish out of water as he stood in the foyer. He was sure everyone would spot him for the fake that he was. Trying to look confident as he would waiting on the first tee, he did not respond when a tall, imposing-looking man in a smart uniform, with a huge red nose, called 'Drummond!'

'Are you asleep, boy?' the man, now standing in front of him, demanded in an English accent. 'Take the cases to room 176.'

With a start, Tommy remembered that he would be called by his master's surname. He took the room key from the man then picked up Hector's and Lavender's suitcases and followed them to the stairway.

'Don't leave this here!' the man's parade ground voice could be heard by everyone in the foyer.

Tommy turned to see him kick his scuffed suitcase, causing it to fall flat, the catch springing open. Aware of a formally dressed party of Americans laughing at him, he rushed back and put down the other cases.

'You'd better smarten up or I'll blacken your other eye,' the man hissed less audibly, looming over Tommy as he scrambled to close his case without revealing its shabby contents. Holding the key in his mouth and his case under one arm, he picked up the other two suitcases and ran to the stair where Hector and Lavender were stifling nervous giggles.

Once the door of their palatial room had been closed, Hector and Lavender shook with mirth. 'Sorry,' Hector wheezed, seeing mutinous resentment on Tommy's face. 'Sorry. You have my permission to laugh the next time I miss a short putt.'

Gradually, a smile came to Tommy's face. 'You're some man, sir. I'll need to remind you that you said that afore you break your putter on me. That man told me he'd give me anither black eye,' he added.

'He'd have me to answer to if he tried,' Hector assured him. 'Here, have a swig of this.' He offered Tommy his hip flask. The caddie needed no second invitation, taking three good swallows of Hector's favourite malt whisky. 'Save some for me, will you,' Hector said. 'The drinks here cost a fortune.'

He continued, 'I think you should stay here meantime, darling. I'll wander about and see if I can spot Haversham and Maxwell. I know Haversham slightly as I was returning officer at last year's election and could reasonably join him.'

'I'd rather come with you.'

'But our cover story is that you need a break. You should be up here, resting. If I think it might help, I can always come and get you. Tommy, or Thomas I should say, you see the head porter and he'll tell you where you are to sleep. I hope you'll be able to get to know Haversham's valet. See if the man has any guilty secrets.'

'Do you mean does he have a fancy woman in London?'

'That sort of thing. Anything, really.'

'Right, sir. That whisky made me feel better. What do I do tomorrow?'

'Get up early and be ready for anything. Take your lead from Haversham's valet, if possible.'

12

As nonchalantly as he could, Hector wandered about the public rooms on the ground floor. There was no sign of Haversham and Maxwell in the bar or the dining room and he began to fear the expedition would be a waste of time. At last, in the lounge, he spied his prey. Haversham was sitting with a man he assumed was Maxwell at a table with no other guests nearby. Blue smoke curled around them. On the wall above, a huge mural depicted Robert the Bruce on his pony defeating the heavily armed English champion, Henry de Bohun, at Bannockburn. It gave Hector hope. There was something of David and Goliath about his own struggle.

'Oh Haversham, fancy seeing you here,' Hector said, advancing on them. 'Mind if I join you?'

From the look on Maxwell's face he did mind, but before he could say anything Hector offered them a drink. 'I see you're both on whisky. Have you tried the Glenturret? It's from Crieff so it's the local malt.' He summoned a waiter with a wave and ordered three large Glenturrets then sat down in a vacant armchair and smiled. 'Have you recovered from the "Flapper Election"?' he asked Haversham. 'Must be odd to see a Socialist in Number Ten.'

Haversham was a tall, thin man with dense, wiry hair that had not retreated but turned completely white. His sharp,

handsome features were spoiled by yellow teeth and a purple
growth on his lower lip. He was too much the politician not
to welcome the returning officer at his count. He took a puff
of his curved Meerschaum pipe and pointed the stem at Hector. 'Certainly it's a shock, but we're taking stock for the next
one. Some people blame all these new woman voters for what
happened last year, but I think we have to respect the elector-
ate and make sure we have the right policies. By the way, do
you know Brian Maxwell? Brian, this is Sheriff Drummond. His
court is in Cupar and his area covers St Andrews.'

Maxwell, who had been frowning at Hector, pulled his
fleshy lips into a synthetic smile. Through a haze of expen-
sive-smelling cigar smoke, his dark eyes assessed Hector, who
was aware of a powerful, almost menacing, physical presence. Maxwell was not only big but also muscular, his biceps
bulging the sleeves of his white tuxedo, his thighs filling his
trouser legs. His brown hair was cut very short, his lumpy
face burned by the sun. Hector thought his head resembled a
hunk of red granite. The bone-crushing handshake came as
no surprise.

'Pleased to meet you, Sheriff,' he said in the nasal twang of
Boston, his voice oddly squeaky.

'Pleased to meet you. I think you were playing in the
Amateur?'

'Correct, but I had some bad breaks Wednesday morning.
I hate these third-rate holes round the loop. They cost me the
match. I guess I'll have to leave this one to Bobby.'

It would take more than a few bad breaks to explain a six
and four defeat, Hector thought, and he's implying a familiarity
with Bob that exists only in his imagination. He said, 'I had bad
luck myself. I found a body in the whins on the second and felt
I had to concede the match.'

'I heard about that. Is it in the rules that you concede if you find a stiff? I'd have carried on.'

'We're probably more sensitive over here. So are you just enjoying a bit of relaxation before you head home, or is business keeping you here?'

Hector saw Haversham nod at Maxwell.

'Pleasure and business. I can't escape my responsibilities. And yourself?' Maxwell asked.

Glad that Lavender had insisted on coming, Hector said, 'My wife has had a difficult time recently and needs a break. She's resting now, but I need a drink. Cheers.' He added a splash of water to the glass newly placed in front of him and raised it. 'To a worthy winner of the Amateur Championship.'

'As I'm British, I hope it might be Roger Wethered,' Haversham said, raising his glass.

Maxwell blew cigar smoke in Hector's direction.

'What line of business are you in?' Hector asked Maxwell, taking a cigarette from his case and flicking his lighter.

Once again, Haversham nodded.

'You could say real estate.' Maxwell replied, his eyes intimidating as they stared at Hector.

'Actually, it's a bit of luck that you should have joined us,' Haversham said, leaning forward. 'Brian has been telling me about a wonderful plan he has for St Andrews.' Maxwell sat back, still staring at Hector. Haversham continued, 'I don't know if you have heard, but the Town Council have made some unwise investments and the town is practically bankrupt. The rates will be bound to go up by so much that half the businesses will close and a lot of residents will have to leave. It's been kept very quiet, but I can't overstate the seriousness of the situation. Fortunately Brian is going to save the town, if he's allowed to do so. He wants to buy the golf courses and build a clubhouse and hotel on the Bruce Embankment. Think of the employment that will bring! We're just fortunate that he should have come along with his scheme at such a difficult moment. Of course there will be those who will resist, but we must not allow them to spoil things for the majority. I hope you, as the respected local sheriff, will help to persuade the doubters. What do you think?'

'I knew some people have had their fingers burnt, but I hadn't realized that the town was in trouble. That's terrible, terrible.' Hector wasn't sure how he should react. By pretending ignorance he was buying time.

'The council took what appeared to be good advice at the time, but it turned out badly. No one could have foreseen it,' Haversham said. 'Until recently there were hopes of a recovery but they've been dashed.'

'But selling the courses, that's drastic.'

Haversham nodded. 'It is, but drastic measures are going to be necessary.'

'Won't you need an Act of Parliament to allow this to go through? I thought the present set-up was written in tablets of stone some time during the last century.'

'That's why Brian has taken me into his confidence.' He puffed at his pipe, self-satisfied. A statuesque lady, tall, broad and well-upholstered with a delicately pretty face passed by, waving aside the smoke with disdain. Hector noticed that Maxwell's dark eyes followed her closely as she left the lounge.

He asked, 'Didn't the Act lay down that the Old Course must be available, free, to all members of the public? What's the point of owning it if you can't charge for playing?'

Maxwell leaned forward and pointed his cigar at Hector as if it were a gun. 'That's the most cock-eyed, socialist bullshit I've ever come across. I love Scotland; my grand-daddy came from Elgin. He went to America to make his fortune, and he

did. Through hard work and enterprise. This wonderful country is being ruined by socialism and my grand-daddy must be
turning in his grave. I plan to do something about it. The Old
Course is the most famous golf course in the world, period. But
it's outdated, not fit to hold a modern championship. I intend to
take in some ground on the New Course and make big changes
round the loop, oh and turn that dip on eighteen you call the
Valley of Sin into a big, deep sand trap. Then it would be both
old and great. You have to pay to play every other course worth
a damn. Why should any hobo with a cleek he's found in a ditch
get to play the Old Course? It's crazy. All the more need for a
new Statute.'

Hector couldn't let this go unanswered. 'It's not about
hobos. It's the birthright of citizens of St Andrews to play their
course for nothing. The Old Course is totally natural and needs
no changes. God made us all equal at birth and at death. In
between we're equal before the law and on the golf course. The
ability to pay should not affect people's right to play our great
game. It's a glorious sight, looking out of the Big Window of the
R and A, a whisky in your hand, and seeing a group of caddies
finishing their rounds in near-darkness, all with fine, natural
swings and a delicate touch on the greens they learned as boys.'
He paused, hoping he had been right to show the depth of his
passion.

Maxwell snorted and sucked at his cigar.

Haversham smiled at Hector. 'The caddies have other
courses in St Andrews to play. If Brian's plan is approved the
hotel/club will bring wealthy visitors to the town and the caddies will be much better off than they are now. And if the rates
go sky-high and St Andrews becomes a ghost town, they might
be able to play the Old Course for nothing but they'll starve. It
really is that serious.'

'We don't need another hotel in town,' Hector said.

Maxwell blew out an enormous cloud of smoke. 'That's where you're wrong, Sheriff. The hotels in St Andrews are old-fashioned and shabby. Compare them to this place. Look.' He stretched his arm, indicating the plush carpet, smart modern tables and chairs and imposing light fittings. 'The hotel I aim to build for St Andrews will have bedrooms with their own bathrooms. The plumbing will work. The heating will work. The food will be great. Wealthy folks will come to the town and spend their money. They'll be happy to pay to get to play my re-designed Old Course. We'll have a professional to give lessons and keep a well-stocked shop. And locals will want to be members of our club because that way they'll be able to play the Old whenever they damn well like. Everyone will be winners. Well, nearly everyone. There sure will be more winners than losers.'

'What about the R and A? They maintain the Old now.'

'That burden would be lifted from their shoulders. But they would have to pay in order to play.'

'And whether they could have the course for their competitions …'

'Would be up to the management of the hotel/club. But I'm sure they would be reasonable.'

Hector was not so sure. By limiting the club's ability to play the Old, altered or not, Maxwell would be able to strangle the R and A and gain revenge for being refused membership. He tried another tack. 'But the Bruce Embankment has to be retained or the view of the West Sands will be spoiled.'

'This hotel would look great anywhere. Mine wouldn't be as big, but it would have the same French chateau look. Once folks have gotten used to it, it will be a fine part of the landscape. Majestic.'

Hector was appalled by what he had heard and saw no point

in pretending otherwise. He said, 'I think it would look vulgar and intrusive.'

'Well I sure hope the rest of the townsfolk can recognize a good deal when it's offered to them. Say, do you still write with quill pens and send convicts to the colonies?' Disdain and contempt on his face, Maxwell sat back in his chair.

It was a long time since Hector had been mocked so blatantly. He stubbed out his cigarette and swallowed the last of his drink.

'I'm sure it will all work out well in the end, Drummond.'

Haversham's attempt to mollify him simply fuelled his anger, greater because it was impotent. 'Some things are best left alone, but I don't expect either of you to understand that,' was his parting shot. He strode out, tears from the smoke running down his face. Lest it should be misinterpreted, he did not take out a handkerchief until he was unobserved.

*   *   *

'So what have you achieved?' Lavender demanded, sitting up in bed an unread book in front of her, tears of anger and distress not far away. 'You haven't learned anything new, they know you're against them, your golf course looks as if it will be sold then altered and Jake is still in prison, facing a murder charge.'

'Sorry, old girl. It looks as if things are stacked up against us, and I don't know what to do.'

'Maybe you should forget about your golf course for a bit and concentrate on Jake's case. I've been saying all along that we should be looking closer to home.'

'I wonder if Tommy has achieved anything,' he said, more in hope than expectation. 'I suppose I should call him to help me undress but I don't think I'll bother.'

13

Tommy had followed a porter about his own age, instructed by the head porter to take him to his room. 'I'm lucky to have this job. I'm no' saying a word against Mr Bailey,' the lad said when Tommy asked how he liked his work.

'Is Mr Bailey the big Englishman with the red nose?'

'Aye. He rules us with a rod of iron. But he's fair. We have to hand over all the tips, but he gives us a share when the hotel shuts for the winter.'

'Does he not keep most of it?'

'He says not. No one knows for sure.'

They had reached the end of the longest corridor Tommy had ever seen and now turned into another, slightly shorter, one. The doors were closer together and the wallpaper less ornate. When they came to a flight of stairs they climbed to the third floor. The ceiling was lower and the walls painted off-white. They came to a room which the porter opened without a key and turned on the light. It contained two single beds, a washbasin, a chest of drawers and two wooden chairs, on one of which dark trousers and a jacket had been neatly laid out. Thin curtains covered the window. From the bed furthest from the door a mop of blond hair protruded. 'You're sharing with Haversham,' the porter said. Tommy looked round the room and placed his case on the nearest bed. He turned to ask the porter where the lavatory was but he had gone. Unsure about what to do next, Tommy put his case beside the chest and sat on the end of his bed.

'Hello, I'm Haversham.' The owner of the blond hair was sitting up, blinking. He was pale, with a sharp nose and eyes wide apart. He wore a shirt without a collar and spoke with the nasal tone of the West of Scotland. Tommy guessed they were of similar age.

'I'm Drummond,' Tommy replied, feeling ridiculous once more.

Haversham made to get back under the covers.

'Most folk call me Tommy. Sorry if I woke you,' he said, mindful of his mission.

The real valet didn't move then sat up. 'I'm Bert. It's a good idea to get forty winks when you can. Never mind. I'm awake now. How long are you here?'

'Just till tomorrow, I think, but I'm no' sure. What about you?'

'The same. I'll see my mum tomorrow. She's in Glasgow, you know. Mr Haversham's going to his home in Fife and he willnae need me till next week, in London.'

Bert was happy to tell Tommy about his life in London as the valet to an important MP, how he lived in a big house in Kensington, and how good Mr Haversham was about letting him stay with his widowed mother when he was at home in his constituency. Mr Haversham's home was just outside Boarhills, a village south of St Andrews. Tommy had visited it once as a child, on an outing organised by a bossy lady with a posh voice who had told him off for trying to get two ice creams. Bert spoke quickly and nervously, smiling often as if for approval. 'What about you?' he asked.

'I'm with Sheriff Drummond. His wife needs a rest so he decided to take her here for a night.'

'Just one night?'

'Aye. Daft-like if you ask me. They had to get away from St Andrews. Her son's been charged with murder and she's gone to pieces a bit.'

'Murder?'

'Aye, murder. Two murders, but Mrs Drummond thinks he's no' guilty.'

'What do you think?'

'It's no' for the likes of me to think.' Normally frank, Tommy was happy to hide behind the sort of thing he thought a valet would say. He considered Jake to be a spoilt brat, but, for the sake of the sheriff and Mrs Drummond, he hoped his name would be cleared. 'I dinnae think the sheriff has any real idea whit he's going to do. They just needed to get away, as I said.' Changing the subject, he asked, 'In London, have you met Mr MacDonald?'

'I've seen him plenty of times, but he's no' in Mr Haversham's party so I've no' been close to him. I've served Mr Churchill at table. He's some man. Talks funny, you know, and he can put it away.'

'Put what away?'

'Drink, of course. He loves a good brandy, I can tell you. He says some awful funny things at dinner. One evening he threw down his spoon and said, "this pudding has no theme".' Bert pronounced "this" and "has" with a slight hiss and paused after "pudding". 'It was cook's special steamed treacle sponge with chocolate sauce and when she heard what he'd said she went in the huff for a week.'

'Whit was the pudding like?'

'It wisnae chocolate and it wisnae a proper steamed pudding either. Like the man said, it had nae theme.' He laughed, a nervous hiccup of a laugh.

'So you get to see a lot of important men?'

'Aye. Mr Haversham's always busy in the evenings. If it's no' parliament or dinner it's cards. He loves his cards. Just as well he's rich because they play for more money in an evening than you and I will see in a lifetime.'

'Does he lose often?'

Bert shrugged as if he had already said too much.

'I bet there are some right fancy women in London?'

'Maybe.'

Tommy tried another tack. 'Why are you here for just one night?'

'Mr Haversham's got awful friendly with an American gentleman. They're going to play golf tomorrow and I think they're planning something.'

'What would they be planning?' Tommy tried not to sound too keen.

'Some project. I heard them mention St Andrews. Don't tell anyone I told you that. They sort of lowered their voices when I was around and Mr Haversham usually doesn't care what I hear. "I know you're discreet, Bert," he often says, but you know what it's like below stairs. Anyway, he's showing off his knowledge of whiskies so I may no' be needed later. But I'd better try and get some sleep in case.'

Tommy wondered why any normal person should need help in getting to bed. Bert gave him directions to the bathroom. When he returned Bert was under the sheet once more. He quickly took off his jacket and trousers and managed to unfasten the collar without too much difficulty. He tried to lay them on his chair as Bert had done, turned off the light and climbed between the cold sheets of his bed. As sleep came to him, he relived Mrs Drummond's soft touch on his face. He imagined he smelt her delicate perfume and ... he stopped himself.

*   *   *

Tommy came to suddenly. The light was on and the porter who had showed him to the room was standing over him. Bert was scrambling out of bed. 'Make it quick,' the porter said and left.

'What's happening?' Tommy asked.

'I've been called.' Tommy saw Bert's hands shook as they did up his fly buttons. Despite the tremor in his fingers, he fastened his collar easily then put on his shoes and jacket and checked his appearance in the mirror on the chest. He rushed out of the room, leaving Tommy to get out of bed and switch off the light.

Curious, Tommy tried to keep awake until his new friend should return but as time passed he dozed off.

*   *   *

Aware of a sniffing sound from Bert's bed, Tommy stirred, cursing himself for not staying awake. Early morning light was spilling through the thin curtains. Curled up, his face to the wall, Bert was quietly sobbing under the covers. His clothes had been carelessly thrown onto his chair. Tommy hesitated.

'What's wrong, Bert?' he asked.

'Nothing.'

'Something is.'

'Nothing. Leave me alone.'

'Did something happen to you?'

'No.'

'Have you been dismissed? Has someone died?'

'No.'

'Then stop greeting and let me sleep.' Tommy turned on his side, facing the door, wondering how he might persuade Bert to talk. He guessed what might have taken place and knew it would be like drawing teeth to get Bert to admit it. 'It happened to me,' he said quietly. 'No' the sheriff,' he added quickly. 'You feel right ashamed.'

He was aware of Bert sitting up in bed. 'Aye, it's the shame of it,' he said quietly.

'Can you no' get another job?'

In the silence that followed Tommy thought Bert was going to clam up but he said, 'No' with the reference he'd give me. And he pays for my mum's treatment. She's no' well. And he gives me time with her when he's in his constituency.'

'But ...'

'It doesn't happen that often. He's very careful in London. There's other staff in the house. And he doesn't take me to his home where his wife is.'

'There must be someone you could tell?'

'I'd be as guilty as him. Think what would happen to me in jail. How did it happen to you?'

'Someone forced me.'

'Right. Just the once?'

'Aye.'

'Did you tell the police?'

'They got to know. He'd done other things. It didnae get to court.'

Bert hugged his knees. 'He sort of forces me. I don't want to do it. He likes to hurt me.' Wincing, he moved so that he lay on his side, facing Tommy. 'My bum's sore,' he said.

Tommy looked at him steadily. 'You cannae let him carry on doing this to you. Let me tell the sheriff. He's a good man and he'll see you don't get into trouble. I'm sure he'd write you a reference if you needed it.'

A flicker of hope on Bert's face was wiped away by doubt.

'It wouldn't work. Mr Haversham's too powerful. His sort gets away with things. And what about my mum's treatment?'

Tommy had no real answer to that. 'But your mum would be raging if she knew what you were doing for her.'

Bert shook his head. 'Na. I'm better off as I am. But thanks. I hear people up. We'd better be ready in case they want an early breakfast. All right if I go to the bathroom first?' As he went out, Tommy noticed a bloodstain on his shirt-tail.

Ten minutes later they were both dressed and ready. 'We just wait here till the porter calls us,' Bert explained. They lay silently on their beds, each thinking his own thoughts.

14

Bert was called first and he returned three quarters of an hour later. Tommy had still not heard from Hector.

Bert said, 'He's playing golf with Mr Maxwell this morning. I had to get his clubs and give them to his caddie. Some job, that! Imagine getting paid for carrying a bag of golf clubs round a field! The lad didnae look the full shilling, if you ask me. Probably got hit on the heid by a ball too often.'

Tommy resisted the temptation to tell him all that a caddie had to do. He was amazed how his new friend appeared to have got over what had happened to him the previous night.

Bert continued, 'So I'm to pack for him and look after his cases. Mr Maxwell's going to give him a lift to his home and then I'll be free to go and see my mum.'

'So Mr Maxwell's going to St Andrews?'

'I suppose so. Why are you interested?'

'No reason.'

Bert gave him a puzzled look. 'Are you sure you're a valet? I'd be in trouble if I reported for work looking like you. Your trousers are creased because you didn't fold them right, your collar's up on one side and your tie's all slack and squint. You have a black eye and you look as if you're outside a lot. You're as brown as that caddie.'

It was now or never, Tommy sensed. He wished he had been

able to tell the sheriff what he had learned, but he would have to follow his own instincts. 'I'm helping the sheriff,' he began. 'We believe Mr Haversham and Mr Maxwell are doing something criminal. The sheriff will help you, but you will have to be prepared to tell what Mr Haversham has been doing to you.'

'So you're a spy?'

'No.'

'Yes. And I've blabbed my secret to you.'

'You can trust the sheriff.'

'Says you.'

'But you can't let this carry on.'

'That's my business, not yours. I have a roof over my head, good food and my mum gets help. When I leave I'll get a good reference. I'm no' going to throw that away.'

'They may have murdered two men, or had them murdered.'

'Another reason not to get involved. I dinnae want to end up wi' my throat cut. Being brave disnae pay for the likes of you and me. My dad was brave, one of the first out of the trenches in the War, one of the first to be shot. I wis only four when he died. I cannae remember him.'

'Why did you talk about having your throat cut? Have you heard something?'

'I'm no' saying any more. Leave me alone. Please don't say what I've told you.'

You're pathetic, Tommy thought. How can I persuade you to speak up for yourself, fight back? Before he could try again the door opened. 'Drummond, you're wanted now,' the porter said.

Bert had turned his back. 'Sometimes you've just got to do what's right,' Tommy said.

'Please don't make my life difficult,' Bert replied, his voice catching.

Tommy shook his head and went to see the sheriff.

*   *   *

'I managed to dress myself,' Hector told Tommy when he arrived at their room, 'but I thought I'd better send for you to keep up the pretence.' He smiled weakly. Lavender stood looking out of the window and did not greet him.

Sensing that they had achieved nothing, Tommy said, 'I think I've got something.' Lavender turned sharply and he could see she had been crying. Sitting on an elegant chair with cushioned seat and arms, he told them everything about his night. 'But he willnae complain, and I don't see him changing his mind. He's got too much to lose.'

'We'll have to change his mind for him,' Hector said grimly. 'Well done, Tommy. I'm afraid we drew a blank. I told Maxwell and Haversham what I thought of their scheme so they know we're against them. Do you think this boy, Bert, will tell Haversham what he said to you?'

'No sir. I'm sure he'll keep his mouth shut and just hope we do nothing.'

'Which we're not going to do. But first, breakfast. I hear you get a jolly good one. Have you had yours?'

'No sir.'

'Well off you go and meet us back here at ten. You'll be coming back to pack for us, well in theory at least. Oh, and keep your eye on Bert.'

'Wait,' Lavender commanded. 'In here.' She took Tommy's arm and led him into their bathroom. As he wondered at the palatial marble and the grand bath, she straightened his collar and tie, pulled at his trousers so they didn't look too big, applied a comb and pomade to his hair and lastly rubbed ointment into his bruised face. His nose twitched as he inhaled another whiff of her heavenly floral scent. In the large mirror above the basin he saw she was looking at him with a weak, half-amused smile. Feeling guilty, he turned away from the reflection.

*   *   *

'Bert's in our room now, packing,' Tommy said urgently. It was nearly half past ten. Hector and Lavender had been waiting restlessly in their room, wondering what was keeping the lad.

'Mr Haversham and Mr Maxwell went to play the King's at half past eight and their car is coming at half past eleven. Bert's been hanging round the foyer, chatting to the porters. He's left Mr Haversham's cases with them. If we go now we'll get him on his own, sir.'

'I think this is a job for Tommy and me,' Hector said. Lavender's face showed her disappointment but she didn't argue. Taking back stairs to reduce the risk of being seen, Hector followed Tommy to the room he had shared with Bert. 'I'm going to be tough on him,' Hector warned before Tommy opened the door. They were just in time as Bert was closing his suitcase and preparing to leave.

'Bert, this is Sheriff Drummond ...' Tommy began.

'You devil, you've telt on me,' Bert hissed, his face showing anger and fear. He clenched his fists and Tommy prepared to fight but Bert restrained himself and stood looking at the floor, his shoulders slumped.

'Sit down, Bert,' Hector commanded.

Not raising his eyes, he perched on the end of his bed, facing Hector.

'What's your surname?'

'Wilson, sir.'

'You know why we're here, Wilson. You and Mr Haversham

have carried out disgusting and illegal acts. I want you to tell me what you told Addison, here, about that.'

Bert continued to look at the floor and said nothing.

'I give you my word, it would be better for you to tell me the truth now.'

No response.

'Very well, you leave me no alternative. I shall telephone the local police who will come immediately. The first thing they will do is have you intimately examined by a police doctor. I am confident that they will find injuries on your body, injuries that will tell their own sordid tale. Mr Haversham's clothes and bedclothes will be seized and more evidence will be found by a careful search. Together with Addison's evidence, there will be a watertight case against both you and Haversham. You will both go to jail, and you can imagine what might happen to you there. It's not a pretty prospect.'

Bert remained quite still, as if he'd been frozen.

'I'm sorry, Wilson, but it's my duty. I have given you an opportunity to make things better for yourself. Addison, stay with him and make sure he doesn't move.' As Tommy tensed himself, Hector turned towards the door but as he turned the handle, a small voice said, 'He forced me, sir.'

Hiding his relief, Hector went back and sat on the end of Tommy's bed, facing Bert. 'Well tell me everything and I swear I'll do my best for you.'

'Will I still have to go to jail, sir?'

'If things work out the way I want them to, you won't even have to go to court.' Seeing the light in Bert's eyes, he qualified that. 'Of course there can be no guarantees, but if you tell the truth now, I will do all I can for you.'

Suspiciously, Bert tried to read the sheriff's face.

Tommy interjected, 'You can trust the sheriff. I telt you he's a good man. I wouldnae have breathed a word of what you said if I didnae think he'd help you.'

Hector, inwardly moved, continued to look stern.

Close to tears, Bert whispered, 'All right. But I dinnae like saying it.'

From his inside pocket, Hector produced some sheets of hotel writing paper and his fountain pen. He placed Tommy's suitcase on his knees and prepared to write down what Bert had to say.

Clearly embarrassed and distressed, Bert began hesitantly but soon the words came in a rush. Hector had to slow him down and seek clarification when confusion or reticence made the narrative disjointed. Outwardly calm as he wrote, Hector seethed at the callous way the MP had inflicted his perverted lust on his compliant but unwilling valet, abusing his body, his dignity and his self-esteem. Half an hour passed before he read out the catalogue of obscene bullying. Shaking, the boy signed each sheet of paper, causing Hector to wince as he pressed the nib of his pen into the page.

Hector got up, folded the papers and put them into his inside pocket. He said to Bert, 'Well done. You need not feel ashamed of yourself. One thing, does anyone else know about this?'

'No sir.'

'Good. Now, go downstairs, act as normal, see Haversham off and then go with Tommy. You can help him take our cases down, saying we'll give you a lift to the station. The porters will think that odd, but by then it won't matter what they might think.'

Bert gave him a wide-eyed look then left. Hector said to Tommy, 'Follow him downstairs and don't let him out of your sight. A frightened rabbit is liable to do some very silly things.'

*   *   *

If Lavender was pleased to hear that Bert was going to help them, she didn't show it. Her only concern was for Jake and she didn't share Hector's conviction that the murders were linked to the attempt to take over the golf course. She paid no attention to the telephone call that he made from the room and appeared distracted when he outlined his plan to thwart Maxwell. When Tommy and Bert arrived, she greeted them half-heartedly.

Tommy was downcast. 'There was a telephone call for Mr Maxwell when they came in from their golf. After he took it he looked as pleased as Punch. I suppose the council must have voted to sell the courses. Mr Haversham looked happy too when they drove away.'

'That's what I expected,' Hector said. 'Now we're going to visit an old school friend, who's a doctor in Perth. He's done work for the police and he's going to examine you, Bert. It won't be pleasant but it is necessary. I've spoken to him on the tele-phone and he's expecting us in an hour's time so we'd better shake our stumps.'

For a moment Hector thought Bert might make a run for it. Tommy though so too and moved to block the door, but the boy's compliant nature showed itself; he shrugged and picked up a suitcase.

It did not take long to pay the bill and load up the car. Bailey, his nose less red than the night before, made a great show of assisting Lavender into the front passenger seat then rushed round to help Hector, who was too quick for him and was already behind the wheel. A false smile creasing his coarse skin, he said he hoped to see Hector again, getting a curt nod in return. In his mirror, Hector saw Bailey and Tommy exchang-ing some words, the false smile turning to a furious glare.

'Tommy, what did you say to that dreadful fellow?' Hector asked as he steered the car down the impressive drive.

'I said, "There'll be nae tips fur you, ye fat-arsed Englishman," – beg pardon, Mrs Drummond.'

'Well done,' Hector said. Lavender and Bert both smiled.

*   *   *

Dr Henry Fallon, Hector's old school friend, was waiting for them when they reached his house, a solid, stone-built property on high ground to the east of Perth overlooking the Tay. Hector had a few words with him then introduced him to Bert, who plainly wished the ground would swallow him. Matter-of-fact and sympathetic, Fallon tried to put him at ease then took him to his surgery, his wife Janet offering sherry to Hector and Lavender. In response to Hector's nod towards Tommy, she offered him some as well. When the drinks arrived, two were paler than the third. If Tommy was aware that he was getting only cooking sherry it did not bother him. They sat in the drawing room, chatting to Janet while waiting for the examination to be over.

Three quarters of an hour passed before Fallon and Bert joined them. Fallon handed a sheet of paper to Hector and asked to speak to him outside. Bert stood awkwardly, blushing and upset.

In the hall Fallon told Hector, 'Clear evidence of internal and external injury within the last twenty-four hours. It must have been painful so I'd be prepared to say it can't have been consensual. There was some scarring as well, indicative of previous episodes. I've applied some ointment, but we can leave it to Mother Nature to heal in time. I've advised him what he should do. It's all down in writing for you. The boy's very scared and nervous. I wouldn't be confident that he'll make a good witness. That man Haversham's a disgrace. I hope you'll make him suffer for what he's put that boy through.'

'I certainly intend to put a spoke in his wheel. This afternoon. Thank you, Henry. Now we must be on our way.'

Ten minutes later they were back in the car, Janet having prepared rounds of sandwiches to sustain them. Tommy was the only one with a healthy appetite.

It was mid-afternoon when they arrived back at Ballochmyle. In the car, Bert had meekly accepted that he should stay with Hector until Haversham had been confronted. His mother had not expected him in Glasgow; he had been going to surprise her. By contrast, Mrs Alves' horror when told that this common boy from Glasgow should occupy Jake's room was obvious. Lavender had ordered this arrangement because the spare room, out of bounds to the girls, contained some of her finest pieces of furniture and was reserved for special guests.

Tommy, under instruction to keep an eye on Bert until Hector returned, took the valet off to weed the vegetable patch; Tindall the gardener suffered from a bad back and Hector, surreptitiously, had been going out of an evening to uproot the most obvious invaders.

'This is another job for me alone,' Hector told Lavender as he prepared to drive away again.

'Well do try to concentrate on the murders. If we don't find out something to help Jake, this will have been a colossal waste of time and to hell with your golf courses.' Her voice caught and she turned away abruptly.

His stomach knotted, Hector got into his car. As he drove, he rehearsed what he would say to Haversham.

15

Grateful for the helping east wind, PC Graham Gemmell ped-
alled his bicycle up the slight incline of Hepburn Gardens on his
way to interview Freddie Torkington. He was unusually nervous. On the one hand, he respected Sheriff Drummond and
did not want to see an innocent person convicted, particularly
if a hanging might ensue. On the other, he was ambitious. He
knew Inspector McTaggart regarded him well, but McTaggart
was autocratic and would not tolerate maverick activity in a
high-profile case. He had already stuck his neck out further
than was wise. Life as a bobby, as policemen were called, was
easy and pleasant enough but Gemmell often yearned for the
excitement and challenges of a city. He didn't want to end up
like Sergeant McNeill, drinking too much, his brain softened,
seeing his comfortable, undemanding wife as a cross between
an old sofa and a servant. God alone knew what she thought of
him, if she ever did think. Perhaps to her he was like a grumpy
old dog, fine so long as he was fed and watered, his flatulent
presence providing an awkward sort of companionship. If he
stayed, would he and Jessie end up like them, occupying the
same police house, all the energy of their relationship spent?
He shuddered. No, Jessie wouldn't stand for that either. He
needed promotion and as that depended on McTaggart, he
couldn't afford to get on his wrong side.

This week, he couldn't complain about a lack of challenges; it was always going to be busy with the Amateur Championship and Bobby Jones in the field. The two murders made things very difficult and he could do without the problem of divided loyalties. He started to hum 'A policeman's lot is not an 'appy one'.

At least he was going to see Torkington with McTaggart's blessing. The inspector had called a meeting that morning and told him and McNeill that no fingerprints had been found on either murder weapon; the killer had wiped them or protected his fingers with gloves or a piece of cloth. Jake Drummond's prints were on the bottle of port found in a whin bush, but so were a number of others. The findings of the two post mortems were more interesting: both victims had died after having their throats cut. This was hardly news, but the pathologist described how the killer had thrust the knife deep into the left side of the throat before drawing it across and through the tissue, severing vital arteries. He would probably have positioned himself so that blood would not have spurted over him. It was likely that Macmillan and Corbett had been murdered by the same person, probably someone with combat training. McTaggart had not ruled out Jake on that basis: 'Remember that they have a Cadet Force at Glenalmond to give the boys military training. Some idiot of a sergeant-major must have trained these boys how to kill.' Gemmell was less sure; he found it hard to imagine the panicky boy carefully and scientifically killing either victim. Further, the pathologist had found a severe bruise on Macmillan's left temple, inflicted shortly before death. Gemmell had noted that Jake was right-handed. The injuries on Macmillan were consistent with his account. After Jake's hard punch to the side of his head, Macmillan might well have fallen with the left side of his neck uppermost, ready for the murderer's thrust of his own *skean dubh*. Another problem was that given what Corbett had said he'd seen, namely someone beside the eighteenth tee of the Old Course, Jake had no reason to think he was about to blame him, provided that he had told the truth about the route he took. Gemmell's growing conviction that the killer was not Jake was deeply troubling. He had suggested to McTaggart that he should interview some of the men putting on the Himalayas, 'in case they remember seeing or hearing young Drummond' and had been commended for his initiative. But he would have to be careful; he did not want to risk a complaint that he had treated Torkington as a suspect.

He had passed the Y junction with Buchanan Gardens and the Torkington's house was on the left. Hidden from the road by a high wall and fir trees, it was spacious and imposing, although the snowcem was tired and stained. Gemmell leaned his bicycle against the wall beside the front door and rang the bell. The loud, tuneless clang brought a maid who opened it cautiously and peered out. Gemmell recognized her as Daisy, a girl his own age who had lived near his parents' house. He remembered her infectious giggle but now she had what his mother would have called a 'hauden doon' look.

'Hello Daisy, how are you?' he said. 'Is Mr Torkington in?'

Seemingly confused, she stammered, 'I'm not sure if ...' then was interrupted by a grand lady's voice, 'Daisy, who is that?'

'It's Graham Gemmell, ma'am, PC Graham Gemmell. He's a policeman.'

'Well tell him to go to the tradesman's entrance.'

Daisy bit her lip and screwed up her face. 'Sorry,' she mouthed and pointed round to her left.

'Don't worry, Daisy,' Gemmell told her, forcing a smile. He went round to the door at the side of the house, seething and reflecting that the Socialists had a point.

The paint on the door was blistered and peeling. Gemmell waited for it to be answered then knocked loudly. Red-faced, Daisy opened it and let him in. 'She made me wait till you knocked,' she whispered. 'They're in the drawing room.' She led him through the kitchen, where an elderly woman was filleting a trout. Squinting through thick glasses, her face was inches above the flesh. Her shaky hands, dirty nails and the drip at the end of her nose made Gemmell briefly grateful that he was unlikely to be invited to stay for lunch.

The drawing room was elegant but shabby, the curtains faded by the sun and the loose cover on the sofa worn. Occupying a padded upright chair, a small, wiry woman dressed in tweed tilted her head back, the better to look down her sharp nose at Gemmell. She nodded towards a less elegant upright chair, angled to face the sun. Gemmell ignored her and perched on the sofa. From a comfortable-looking arm chair beside the fireplace a grey-haired man smiled at him, apparently unaware of the game that had just been played. 'How may I help you, officer?' he asked.

'I have some questions regarding the murder of Gordon Macmillan. I'd prefer it if we might talk alone.' He looked at Mrs Torkington, raising his eyebrows.

She gave him a chilling glare. 'My husband and I have no secrets.' She settled back in her chair.

I wonder if she knows about his financial troubles, he thought, but said, 'Very well.' Turning to her husband, he asked, 'I understand that, after a dinner in the New Club, you and a number of others were putting on the Himalayas on Sunday evening?'

'Yes indeed.' He nodded his head.

Gemmell found it difficult to take his eyes off Torkington's neck. It was the first time he had seen him at close quarters. The tiny chin and the Adam's apple wobbled about independently of each other; it was hard to say where the neck ended and the jawbone began. Disconcerted, he asked, 'And do you know anything about Mr Macmillan's murder?'

'What do you mean by that, officer?'

'Well, at any time did you see Mr Macmillan?'

'I may have. I honestly can't remember. It had been a jolly good dinner,' he added apologetically. His wife frowned.

'Did you hear any shouting or argument coming from the golf course?'

'After the *haar* came in I did hear shouting. A man's voice and a younger voice. Or voices.'

'What were they shouting?'

'The man was shouting something about "disgrace" or "degenerate" then "needing a thrashing". I couldn't make out what the younger voices were saying.'

'Can you remember hearing anything else, any thumps or cries?'

'No.'

'Apart from the other men putting, did you see anyone coming away from where you heard the shouting, or going towards it?'

'Can't say I did.'

'When the *haar* came in, I believe the putting stopped. What did you do then?'

He shifted in his seat. 'I left, just like the others.'

'Where did you go?'

'I went home, actually.'

'What about the rest of them?'

'I heard one or two saying they'd go back to the New Club.'

'But you didn't join them?'

'No. It was time to call it a day, as far as I was concerned.'

'Who did you walk with when you left the Himalayas?'

'I can't remember. Dammit, why are you asking all these questions? You've got someone in custody, haven't you?'

Aware that Mrs Torkington was becoming increasingly restless, Gemmell tried to calm things. 'We have made an arrest, sir, but it is important that there should be a thorough investigation. We need to know the movements of everyone who was around the scene of the crime. We're not picking on you.' He smiled reassuringly. 'Who did you walk with when you left the Himalayas?'

His chin and Adam's apple twitched as Torkington resisted the temptation to bluster. 'If you must know, I left alone. I'd had a call of nature, so I went into the bushes.' He ignored his wife hissing 'Frederick!' and continued, 'By the time I'd finished the rest had gone. So I went home.'

'By car?' Gemmell couldn't stop himself.

'I was damned careful. I can hold my drink, you know.'

Mrs Torkington's face was now thunderous. She would certainly have something to say when Gemmell left.

'And the bushes you visited for your call of nature, where were they?'

'Just along from the little clubhouse for the Himalayas. Between it and the eighteenth green of the New. Away from the shouting. And I didn't hear or see anything relevant to Macmillan's murder,' he added then scratching his cheek, said, 'Hold on, there was a rum sort of noise, a clank of metal as if someone was cycling away from the Jubilee and going as fast as they could. Damned fool, I remember thinking. The *haar* had become a real pea-souper.'

Was this Jake or Sorley? Gemmell wondered. It supported the boys' version of events. If they had left the scene by way of the Jubilee, on bikes, they would not have been seen by anyone on the Himalayas or the Old Course. He made to get up then sat back. 'Just one more thing, sir. Do you know anything about anonymous letters threatening prominent St Andrews people with bankruptcy?'

Torkington's face coloured and his whole neck became jelly. 'What makes you think I might?'

Gemmell saw the look of incredulity on Mrs Torkington's face. This had come as news to her, news her husband's reaction had confirmed. He hesitated, choosing between going in hard and playing it gently. Remembering promotion, he said, 'It's just a rumour going about, sir. Some say it might be connected with Mr Macmillan's financial advice.'

Torkington had now set his face and neck in stone. 'I can't tell you anything about that. I'm glad to say,' he added, glancing at his wife.

'The rumour has it that these letters were written using mirror writing. Apparently it was used during the War to fool the censors.'

'Well, I was too old for the last show. I did my bit in South Africa. Damned fierce fighters, the Boers. Of course we all heard about mirror writing after the War.' Another glance at his wife told him he had said too much. 'If that's all, officer? Always happy to help the police.'

'Daisy!' Mrs Torkington shouted. 'The policeman's going. Show him out.' Looking away from Gemmell, she lit a cigarette. He noticed that her hand shook as she did so.

16

Passing Corbett's farm on his way, Hector worried that he might not learn anything to Jake's advantage from Haver- sham, even if he did save the golf courses from a take over. Never before during their marriage had he and Lavender been so disconnected; her whole focus was on her son, our son he corrected himself. Had he been guilty of concentrating exclu- sively on Maxwell's scheme at the expense of Jake's plight? His attitude to Jake had been a niggle for years. He had to admit to himself, if no one else, that try as he might, he couldn't truly regard the boy as his own flesh and blood. Lavender sensed it and so did Jake.

Haversham's house was called Fettlegask. Well-bred but impecunious, he had married the plain daughter of a Yorkshire coal-mining family. Round St Andrews it was reputed to be a marriage made not in heaven but under the earth, the sweat and blood of the miners providing the aspiring politician with the money to indulge his pretentious aspirations. By contrast with his extravagant lifestyle, his wife, increasingly reclusive, lived simply and frugally in the grand house he had bought in his constituency.

Hector had not visited Fettlegask for a long time and his memory of it was not happy. Then owned by the Thirlstanes, a half term teenage ball had been held there on a cold February night many years earlier. Hector's best friend, John Taylor-Smith had been staying with him during the Glenalmond half term, and Hector had proudly shown off his girlfriend, Lavender. The three of them had left the smoky fug of the party and walked down a drive lined with skeletal, spooky trees and carpets of snowdrops. It was then that Hector first noticed how the other two laughed at each other's jokes and nudged each other playfully. When they came back into the light, he could see her smiling at John in a way she had rarely smiled at him. In his heart of hearts he knew then that their romance, such as it was, was over. Now he had come to accept that their marriage, though successful, was based on great affection and convenience rather than passion. When John had died in the mud of Ypres, a bit of Lavender had died too. And Jake was a constant reminder of John.

Hector stopped the car outside the entrance gateway of Fettlegask. He had not been back since that night. He did not remember the pair of stone Griffins, ready to pounce on hostile visitors. The skeletal trees were now green and flourishing, the snowdrops long past, their narrow leaves lying flat. Forcing gloomy thoughts to the back of his mind, he concentrated on what he wanted to achieve from the coming encounter.

The leaden feeling in his stomach as he rang the bell was as bad as when he'd led a charge over the top, his cheeks rouged so his men would not realize how scared he was.

A maid answered promptly. 'Good afternoon sir.'

'I'm Sheriff Hector Drummond. I am here to see Mr Haversham. Please tell him the matter is urgent.'

She opened the door for him. 'Certainly sir. Please wait in the hall. Is he expecting you?'

'No, but as I say, the matter is very urgent.'

The maid left him in the wood-panelled hall, virtually

unchanged since that dance. There was a minstrels' gallery and a stained glass window. He remembered lights, music and gaiety. Now it was more like a mausoleum, well kept but dreary. An oil painting of a gloomy-looking man in Victorian dress with Haversham's features was his attempt to make the place his in spirit as well as in law.

'Drummond, my dear chap, what can I do for you?' Haversham's voice jolted Hector. 'I was just taking tea with my wife. Do you want to join us?' Dressed in a tweed suit and smiling, he was the image of a benign country squire.

'There is something I have to say to you alone. It's very important. And urgent.'

'Very well.' Haversham seemed unperturbed. Going to the door from which he had come, he told his wife that he would see the sheriff in his study and led the way across the hall into a room lined with books. Above the fireplace was a painting of Haversham himself, preening himself as a man of destiny. He sat behind the massive desk and offered Hector the chair opposite. Hector noted that he was now lower than his host.

'It's about the proposal to sell the golf courses ...' he began.

'Too late, my dear chap. This morning the town council voted to petition parliament for permission to sell the links. I anticipate that the Joint Green Committee will take the same view next week, but in any event it's the town council that matters. In just over an hour, and in this very room, some journalists I have invited will hear me welcome the vote and pledge to use my influence to make sure the necessary Act is passed. I appreciate that you feel strongly on the issue but I hope you will come to see the considerable advantages of the proposal, and support it.'

'I have been making some inquiries, and I have to tell you that Mr Maxwell does not enjoy a good reputation in the United

States.' He paused to assess the reaction. Haversham raised his eyebrows but seemed unconcerned.

'I don't think it would be a good thing for him to be powerful in St Andrews.'

'I disagree.'

'I am told that he made a fortune illegally, by bootlegging.'

'That's in the past. Prohibition is plain stupid, anyway. It's not like robbing banks.'

'I'm told also that he has made money out of prostitution.'

'Have you any proof? What is the source of your information? All successful men attract envious and malicious rumours.'

'It is undoubtedly the case that he has made even more money by short-selling. He has become rich by taking advantage of other men's weaknesses and ill fortune.'

'That's called capitalism, Drummond.'

'I thought capitalism encouraged enterprise and hard work.'

'There are many facets to it.'

Hector paused, as if thinking about the last remark then said, 'I believe it is unwise to play cards with him for money.'

A flicker of Haversham's eyes told Hector that he had landed a blow. He said nothing.

'Bribery and blackmail are ugly weapons, don't you agree?'

Haversham frowned. Impatiently he said, 'Of course. Now, if you have nothing else to say ...' He rose from his chair.

'Oh but I have. You tried to make big profits by playing the American stock market, but you got in at the wrong time and lost a lot of money. You've lost even more by playing cards with Maxwell. Now you're facing ruin, unless your wife's family bail you out, but are they perhaps tired of doing that?' Glaring at Hector, Haversham sat down. 'Maxwell holds your gambling debts and, after buying debt from the Enright Bank, he holds your stock market debt too. No doubt interest is running at a crippling rate. You are in serious financial trouble but he has thrown you a lifeline: if you support him here in St Andrews and in parliament he'll write off your debt. I am not wrong, am I?'

Haversham's expression confirmed it. Thinking desperately, he said, 'What a lot of nonsense.'

Hector sat back, saying nothing, trying to hold a poker face.

Haversham seemed to collect himself and made to get up again. 'As I said, I'm expecting some journalists soon. I would like you to leave now.'

Hector did not move. Dropping his voice, hoping to add menace to his words, he said, 'Jail trumps bankruptcy.'

'Don't be preposterous, man. I certainly intend to complain about your unspeakable conduct.' Haversham was clearly furious.

'What about your conduct, conduct that dares not speak its name?'

The MP stared at him.

'I have a full, signed statement from your valet, Bert Wilson, listing the unspeakable things you have been doing to him, in London and last night at Gleneagles. The evidence of my man, Addison, and the porter who called him last night will prove you had him in your room. Wilson has been medically examined by an experienced doctor who found internal and external injuries inflicted within the last few hours. He says that what was done to him would not have been done with his consent. There is a very strong case against you and you are likely to be sent to prison for several years. And by God you deserve it.'

Haversham looked as if he had been punched very hard in the stomach. He subsided into his chair. For a full minute neither man said anything then Hector said, 'I hate doing this but I am prepared to give you a way out.'

The MP said nothing but looked inquisitively at Hector.

'The following conditions are non-negotiable.'

Haversham gave the slightest nod.

'First, you will pay Wilson four hundred pounds, and you will give him a glowing reference which I shall dictate to you.'

'Four hundred pounds?'

'Four hundred pounds, and you will be getting away cheaply.'

The MP said nothing.

'Second, you will read out to the journalists you are expecting a statement that I shall also dictate to you. It will kill Maxwell's proposal tone dead.'

Haversham winced.

'Third, you will tell me everything you know about Maxwell's scheme, in particular the late Mr Macmillan's role in it, and whether he had, to your knowledge, any enemies.'

'Of course, you are desperate to get your brat off the hook.' An evil smile briefly lit the MP's face.

Hector kept his temper with difficulty. 'My brat, as you call him, is innocent, unlike you. And believe me, it would give me great pleasure to throw you to the wolves.'

An uneasy silence followed, then Hector said, 'Fourth, you will apply for the stewardship of the Chiltern Hundreds.'

'Resign my seat?' he gasped.

'You are totally unfit for any public office, and you know it. All four conditions must be met. You will announce your resignation to the journalists this afternoon. You can give ill health as the reason.' Hector stared across the desk at a broken man. He wished he could make him feel even worse.

Looking down, Haversham whispered, 'All right.'

'All four conditions, in full?'

He nodded. 'Yes.'

'Well we'd better start.'

Despite his acceptance, Haversham asked, 'What guarantee do I have that I will hear no more of this … allegation?'

'You have my word, as a gentleman.'

'If that's not enough?'

Hector ignored the insult. 'You will be able to accuse me of blackmail. The returned cheque for four hundred pounds will be evidence supporting you. Of course, if you were to get your blow in first and accuse me of blackmail, the whole sorry, sordid truth would come out. If you do as I say, not even your wife need know about Wilson, and I believe she stands to inherit a lot of money one day?'

Haversham said nothing. He averted his eyes from Hector, his mouth twitching as he desperately tried to think how he might rescue his situation.

Hector sat back, looking steadily at him. 'Time marches on,' he said. 'I suggest you get out your chequebook.'

Slowly, Haversham opened a drawer of his desk and produced his chequebook.

'Make it payable to Sheriff H.N. Drummond, in brackets "B W". Four hundred pounds. I will pay it into my bank on Monday and rest assured, Wilson will get the full amount.'

Haversham wrote the cheque and pushed it across the desk.

Hector folded it and put it in his inside pocket. 'Now, on your writing paper: "Bert Wilson has served me tirelessly as my valet. He is loyal, discreet and he knows his job. I am sorry to lose him, and I highly recommend him to any future employer." Now sign and date it,' he added as Haversham finished writing.

The reference was pushed across the desk. Hector checked it and put it in his pocket.

'Now tell me what you know about Macmillan, in particular the relationship between him and Maxwell.'

Haversham turned and, with a sigh, seemed to address one of his bookcases. 'Macmillan was a solicitor who gave financial advice to me amongst others. He advised investing in American stocks, and borrowing to buy as much as possible. It worked for a bit but the crash spoiled things.'

'I know that.'

'Maxwell was introduced to Macmillan earlier this year, I believe by a broker called Feinstein. For a time Macmillan advised Maxwell. He explained the statutory position of the links, for one thing. About Easter I met Maxwell. We played cards and I lost.'

'Heavily?'

A wry smile passed across Haversham's face. 'Yes. Then I was fooled by the dead cat bounce and lost even more on the New York stock exchange. As you seem to know, Maxwell bought the debt I owed to the Enright Bank and, with the gambling debts, he could have ruined me. There is merit in his proposal, you know. If you wreck it the town will face disaster.'

'I don't believe so. What was Macmillan doing all this time? Do you know anything about the anonymous letters that went out recently?'

'Anonymous letters?'

Hector looked at him incredulously. 'Yes, sent to town councillors and members of the Joint Green Committee putting pressure on them to support Maxwell's scheme.'

'I had nothing to do with them. And neither did Macmillan, I'm sure.'

'How do you know?'

'Maxwell had no time for him. He called him prissy and feeble because he refused to continue to act for him. 'Chickenshit' was a phrase I recall. There was a conflict of interest, you see, and Macmillan stayed with his old clients who were about to be sued by Maxwell. Say what you like about him, but the man had some principles.'

'And Maxwell isn't used to people saying no to him?'

'Exactly.'

'So who did write the anonymous letters?'

'I don't know.'

'You must. You and Maxwell have been as thick as thieves.'

Haversham flinched at the comparison. 'I don't know, and I didn't need to know. It was better, easier for me if I knew nothing about any doubtful methods.'

Hector saw his point. 'Do you think Maxwell has an ally in the town?'

'He may have but I don't know. He might have sent the letters himself.'

'Apart from Maxwell, who might have wanted to harm Macmillan?'

'I have no idea. Perhaps someone who had lost a lot of money through following his advice.' Haversham raised his voice. 'I have told you everything, everything.' His face red, he breathed rapidly. Hector hoped he was not about to have a heart attack.

'But why the night at Gleneagles?'

'To make sure we had our arrangements for today coordinated. We drafted out statements for the press. I am to give the first one within the hour then Maxwell will speak to them after dinner.'

'Let me see the one you were supposed to make.'

Haversham took a sheet of paper from the leather folder on his desk and handed it to Hector, who glanced at it. It was written on Gleneagles writing paper. In it the MP welcomed the vote of the town council, praised the proposal and undertook to bring the necessary enabling Bill before parliament as soon as possible.

'Now the one you will make,' Hector said. 'Please write down exactly what I say: "It is the birthright of every St Andrews citizen to be able to play golf on the links, the Old Course in particular, free of charge. This birthright is precious, something to be fought for. The present arrangements are both principled and pragmatic and in 1894 parliament gave them statutory effect. The vote by the town council to try to sell the links is a betrayal of the people of the Royal Burgh. I have no intention of assisting this proposal, which I believe to be deeply flawed. Without an amending Act of Parliament the scheme cannot proceed, and that is a good thing.

"This will be my last service to those who have elected me. Recently I have been under very great strain. My health has suffered to the extent that I must cast aside the burden of public service I have been privileged to bear. I intend to apply for the Stewardship of the Chiltern Hundreds and so leave public life. I simply wish to thank all of those who have placed their trust in me as their Member of Parliament." That's all. Please let me see it.'

After reading it over Hector asked, 'When do the journalists arrive?'

Haversham consulted his pocket watch. 'Within the next ten minutes or so. I said I would make my statement at five, in time for tomorrow's papers.'

'I'll wait and sit beside you while you make it. Don't worry,' he said, seeing Haversham's shocked reaction, 'provided you stick to the script, I'll praise you for your public service over the years.'

They sat in uneasy silence until the doorbell rang. The maid announced that three journalists had arrived together. As she fetched chairs for them, Hector moved his so he could sit at Haversham's elbow. The three filed in, one from each of *The Scotsman, The Dundee Courier* and *The St Andrews Citizen*. In a halting voice, Haversham thanked them for coming and read out the statement Hector had dictated. When he had finished there was silence. Hector could see that, taken aback though they were, they had already worked out the consequences. The representative of *The Scotsman* cleared his throat then asked why he had decided to resign with so little warning. Hector, adopting his most authoritative courtroom manner, cut in before Haversham could say anything and praised the retiring MP for years of public service and hoped he would be allowed privacy at this difficult time. The journalists, curiosity written on their faces, left. The show was over.

After giving the journalists time to drive away, Hector picked up the statement from the desk and got up. 'Goodbye Haversham,' he said.

The defeated man slumped in his chair and said nothing.

17

Squinting as he drove west into the sun, Hector's mind was spinning. Macmillan had changed sides, but how many had known this? His killer might have been in favour of the project and known the situation or been against it and not known. The list of possible suspects had lengthened.

Hector felt confident that he had scuppered Maxwell's project, but the debt problem remained. He needed to confront the American and make sure he did not wreak financial ruin on the town and many of its citizens. He wondered if he should report back to Lavender but she would have been scornful of what he had learned from Haversham. He decided to go to the Grand and see Maxwell there. There would be plenty of time to concentrate on Jake's plight later.

Fortunate to find a parking space on The Scores, Hector walked down to the hotel. He saw a great crowd surging up the eighteenth fairway, the excitement palpable. Engrossed by his problems, he had forgotten the championship. Pushing himself forward to a viewpoint at the top of the R and A steps, he was able to see a player hitting his second from a position over Granny Clark's Wynd, the road crossing the course, and to the left of the fairway from the players' perspective. He recognized Jones' elegant swing. As soon as he hit the ball, the spectators rushed forward. Into the wind, the ball soared up into the sky and landed on the green, finishing a couple of yards from the hole to great applause.

'An amazing match,' the man in the flat cap beside him replied to Hector's query. 'Jones couldnae putt for toffee and wis two down with five to play. Voigt let him back in, but then looked as if he was going to win the seventeenth till Jones holed a tram-liner for a half. Now Voigt's in the Valley of Sin and Jones has that for a birdie.'

Obviously, Jones had beaten England's Eric Fiddian in the morning and his afternoon opponent in the semi-final was his fellow American George Voigt from New York, a formidable adversary. On three consecutive afternoons Jones had faced renowned players, each match going to the eighteenth hole or beyond. His place in the final looked assured when Voigt's run-up from the Valley of Sin finished four feet short. Jones took his putter, Calamity Jane, from Jack McIntyre. The caddie's quick movements as he backed away betrayed his nerves. The crowd fell silent as Jones went through his usual routine and putted for the match. The ball was on line. Those who saw that began to cheer but Jones had under-hit it and it stopped just short of the hole. The cheer turned to a collective gasp of shock and disappointment. Now Voigt only had to hole his four-footer to take Jones down the nineteenth. Hector could barely look as the New Yorker putted but missed. Jones was in the final, only by the skin of his teeth. Temporarily distracted from his mission, Hector made his way through the crowd towards the Grand Hotel. Feeling a tug on his arm, he turned and found Tommy, out of his valet's outfit and wearing his brown, shapeless suit.

'What a match, sir. I thought Mr Jones wis a gonner, right enough.'

'I wish I'd seen more of it. But what are you doing here? Is Bert all right?'

'Och he's fine, sir. He's feart of Mr Haversham and no' of a mind tae move. If he wis, Mrs Alves and Mrs Drummond would see he stays. How did you get on with Mr Haversham?'

'Well. I think I've saved the courses. I just hope I can prevent the town from going bankrupt. But why are you here?'

'I wis sure you'd come here after seeing Mr Haversham and I've heard some bad things about Mr Maxwell. I thought you could do with someone at your back.'

Hector smiled. 'Thank you, Tommy. Let's go,' he said, more grateful than his reaction suggested.

Although the foyer of the Grand was crowded with those who had witnessed the great match, Mary the receptionist was not busy. She beamed when she saw Hector and was happy to tell him, in a stage whisper he wished was less carrying, about Maxwell's latest plans.

'You know I'm not an eavesdropper, my lord,' she began, causing a lady standing nearby to turn sharply, 'but after what you told me, I've been listening in to Mr M's', she winked, 'calls.'

'Yes?' Hector whispered, moving his head closer in the hope of making her speak more quietly.

'Well some gentlemen, mostly town councillors, are coming to meet him at seven-thirty in a private room and he's hosting dinner for them at eight. There will be fifteen of them dining. Imagine the cost of that! Then three journalists are due to meet him in his suite at nine-thirty.'

'That's very interesting. Thank you. Could you tell me where his suite is?'

'It's on the third floor, room 301, on the corner of the hotel, you know with lovely views all round?'

'Yes, I think I do. One more thing, has Mr Haversham telephoned and asked for Mr Maxwell?'

'No, my lord, no.' She shook her head and raised her eye-brows, obviously wanting to know more.

'Well if he does within the next half hour, could you please say the telephone's busy or something. I'd rather they didn't speak to each other right now.' In the car, Hector had cursed himself for not telling Haversham not to tip off Maxwell.

She winked conspiratorially and gave a slight nod.

'Thank you, Mary,' Hector said at normal volume. 'Come on, Tommy.'

As they made their way through the foyer, Bobby Jones, flanked by his wife and O.B., entered the hotel, Jack McIntyre in their wake and carrying the precious clubs. All of them looked as if they had been through an emotional wringer.

'Hey, Hector!' Jones called. When Hector went over to him he said quietly but urgently, 'I heard the news about the course. What's going to happen?'

'It's not so bad, but I can't speak here.'

Jones looked at him appraisingly. 'Well let's all go up to the sitting room on the second floor. I'd sure like to know what's happening.'

Minutes later he had made his way through a swarm of admirers and well-wishers and joined the rest, including Tommy and Jack, still carrying the clubs, in a bright room overlooking the eighteenth green where there was no one to overhear. 'I could sure use a Scotch,' he said and ordered whiskies all round. Hector felt that some Dutch courage would do no harm and was happy to accept.

When the waiter bearing the drinks had gone, Jones took a deep draw on his cigarette and said to Hector, 'You cannot allow that appalling man Maxwell to take over this wonderful golf course. He'll ruin it.'

'That won't happen,' Hector said. 'It would need an Act of

Parliament and I've just had a conversation with Haversham, the MP, who has changed sides.'

'I'm mighty glad to hear that, but how did you make him change his mind?'

Hector hesitated but, emboldened by a swallow of whisky, Tommy blurted out, 'He wis buggering his valet. Oh sorry, Mrs Jones.'

Jones registered surprise then amusement. 'And to prevent that getting out, he ...?'

'Exactly,' Hector said. 'But please don't tell anyone else, Tommy. It wouldn't help for that to become known, at least for a while.'

Tommy was crestfallen. 'Sorry, sir, but I thought I could tell Mr Jones.'

Jones smiled at him. 'Your secret's safe with us, Tommy, Hector. I'm a lawyer back home, and I'm well used to respecting confidences. The same goes for everyone here.'

Briefly, Hector gave a resume of his dealings with Haversham. He concluded, 'So I'm here to persuade Maxwell not to bankrupt the town, but what about you? You've had some testing afternoon games.'

'For some reason the afternoons have been tougher than the mornings. This morning young Eric Fiddian, fine player though he is, waited till the back nine to show his mettle. But that was too late. I was four up at the turn and won by four and three.'

'Then someone told you about that vote by the town council and Maxwell's plans for the course,' O.B. said. 'I've never seen you so quietly angry and upset.'

'When you confirmed that it was true it shook me,' Jones admitted, 'and I nearly let it cost me my afternoon match.'

'By Jove!' Hector was surprised; Jones' powers of concentration were phenomenal.

'I had a long wait after my morning round and I felt tired and nervous. Hector, I want to win this championship so much. I've been dreaming of it for months and here I was in the semi-final, within touching distance. The thought that Maxwell might buy up this course then alter it filled me with horror. Mary and I came up here and we had a glass of sherry. I felt it might steady my nerves. Now I have never before touched a drop of alcohol before a tournament round. I've enjoyed a cocktail or two before a friendly or even an exhibition match, but never before a tournament round. Well, my face was flushed and I was horribly aware that my eyes were the slightest bit out of focus. As our starting time approached and the condition continued I got panicky. I swear that I didn't get that sherry out of my eyes till we were half way round the course.'

'But you holed a fifteen-footer for a birdie at the first,' O.B. pointed out.

'It was going far too hard. If it hadn't hit the back of the hole it would have been a long way past. From then on I missed putts all over the place. I even fluffed a short pitch at the thirteenth. I went to the fourteenth two down.'

'They say, "two up with five to play never wins",' Hector said.

'I've never had any faith in that maxim,' Jones replied, 'and George Voigt is too good a player to let that lead slip easily. But he made a couple of mistakes and I was all square with two to play.'

O.B. said, 'After missing so many, how did you hole that four-yard putt for a half on the seventeenth?'

Jones smiled, thinking how to reply. 'I know it sounds strange, but when I stood up to it, I had the feeling that something had been taking care of me through two matches that I might very well have lost, and that it was still taking care of me. I knew that however I struck that putt, it was going down. Luckily for me, he made a mess of the eighteenth and that was that.'

'Well good luck against Roger Wethered tomorrow,' Hector said, stubbing out his cigarette. 'But Tommy and I have business to attend to. I just hope that the something that has been taking care of you will be looking out for us.'

18

As he climbed the stairs to the third floor, Hector gathered his thoughts. Maxwell would be a tougher nut to crack than Haversham; he would be more used to serious confrontations than the politician, who would have wriggled his way round issues. Moreover, Hector did not have such a strong card to play against him as he had in his hand at Fettlegask. He knew one thing: the slightest sign of weakness on his part would be seized on. It was like confronting a dangerous dog – or the Appeal Court in his days at the bar, when three highly intelligent and vastly experienced old men would rip apart a shoddy argument with the viciousness of a hungry Alsatian attacking a lump of meat.

Sooner than he might have wished, he and Tommy stood in the corridor outside Maxwell's suite.

'I remember it from three years ago.' Tommy spoke quietly, his mouth dry. He had carried out a daring raid then, and the fear he had experienced came back to him. 'You go through this door and you're in a wee dark hallway. The door on the left leads to the sitting room and the door straight ahead goes into the bedroom. There's a door between the two rooms.'

Carefully, Hector tried the first door. It was unlocked and they went into the hallway. 'You wait here,' Hector whispered. He pulled the door shut behind them. They were in almost complete darkness, a glass panel above the door to the corridor providing the only light. There was a smell of stale cigar smoke but no sound from either room until they heard a clink of glass. 'Here we go. Wish me luck,' Hector whispered then knocked on the sitting room door.

'Come!' Maxwell's voice was strong and commanding.

Hector opened the door and stepped in. The room was situated on the rounded corner of the hotel. Its windows gave a panoramic view stretching from the North Sea, across the West Sands and the golf courses, to the row of irregular buildings running up the right of the eighteenth fairway. The American stood with his back to the door, the bulges in his white tuxedo emphasising the physical threat that he presented. He was gazing out over the golf course, a large whisky in one hand, an unlit cigar in the other. He paused before turning to see who had entered. The arrogance of his pose made Hector's determination grow second by second.

'Whaddayawant?' Maxwell snapped, contempt in his voice.

Concealing his irritation, Hector sat down on an upright chair. He crossed his legs and took out his cigarette case. 'I hear you won the vote in the town council today,' he said.

'And soon all this will be mine.' Maxwell waved his unlit cigar in a wide sweep.

'I don't think so.' Hector carefully lit a cigarette and exhaled in the American's direction.

'Whaddayamean?' The contempt was tinged with irritation. He looked at Hector aggressively.

'What I say. I don't think any of what you've been gazing at will ever be yours.'

Maxwell left the window and stood in front of Hector, an unspoken threat of violence in his expression and body language. 'You won't stop me. Back in the States we've a word for folks like you: a punk. There's nothin' about you that frightens me. You live in the past and you've become part of your own history. I live in the future. I can make this place bigger and better and in time the folks of this quaint old town will thank me. I'll be remembered for pulling it into the twentieth century. There's not a thing you can do to prevent me from buying everything I want here then making the changes that I need to make. In Texas they'd say you were "all hat, no cattle". To me you're just a punk.' His squeaky voice subtly added to the menace of his words and attitude.

Feeling vulnerable and wishing he had remained standing, Hector stared up at the red, angry face. He focused on the lumpy, pockmarked nose, hoping to give the impression of looking eye to eye. 'You will not be allowed to buy the golf courses,' he said, managing to keep his voice steady. 'I think I should read you a statement that Mr Haversham made to the press just over an hour ago.' He took the statement from his pocket and began to read. As he did so, Maxwell sat down on a sofa, facing Hector and lit his cigar, his dark eyes narrow and calculating. If he was shaken, he did not show it.

'You're kidding. I don't believe it.' His lips twisted into a sour smile.

'Telephone him and let him tell you himself.'

'I'm gonna do just that. Then you can get outa here.' He reached for the telephone and asked to be connected to Mr Haversham's house. 'Well when it's stopped being busy, put me through … What? … Why yes, he's here … She wants to speak to you.' He handed the receiver to Hector.

'Yes please, as soon as it's stopped being busy,' Hector told Mary. He passed the telephone back to Maxwell and sat back, trying to keep his hand from shaking as he drew on his cigarette.

They sat and smoked in silence, both affecting nonchalant

confidence. When the telephone rang, Maxwell reached for it as if he had all the time in the world.

'Courtney, how did your meeting with the journalists go? … What?' He sat forward. 'Why? … You changed your mind? … Well I'm gonna unchange it for you … What do you mean too late? … Goddamn you. There will be consequences … You will be sorry.' Hector thought he might have broken the receiver as he crashed it down. 'How in hell's name did you pull that off?' he demanded.

'That's none of your concern. But your plan is dead in the water.'

'Not until I say it is. Haversham's gonna change his mind. I'll make sure he does. Now get the hell outa here before I break your neck.' Sitting on the edge of the sofa, his face contorted, the American was shouting. There was nothing false about his fury.

Hector stubbed out his cigarette and prepared to defend himself. Keeping his voice level, he said, 'It's over. Even if Haversham changed his mind, he'd have lost all credibility. It was essential for your scheme that the government listened to him and made parliamentary time for a new Act. That's not going to happen now.'

Maxwell put down his cigar. He stood up and loomed over Hector, fists clenched at his sides, breathing deeply.

'I'm not finished,' Hector said, a curious sensation of devil-may-care recklessness calming him. 'You will leave town by Monday morning, but before you go you will discharge all debts owed to you by St Andrews and its citizens.'

'I don't believe I'm hearing this. Are you crazy?' Hector felt a drop of spittle land on his face.

'No, I'm not crazy. You will do exactly as I say because you don't want to end up in jail. You have been trying to corrupt public figures and I can prove it. That's taken very seriously here. If you doubt it, ask your lawyer about the Prevention of Corruption Act 1906. The penalties are severe. I'm offering you a way out. If you don't take it, I'll see to it that you will be arrested on Monday morning.'

Maxwell's mouth moved but only a grunt came out. He took a step back then paused. Suddenly he launched himself at Hector, causing him to fall backwards. There was a loud crack as his chair splintered beneath him. Before he could react he felt the American's hands round his throat and he was gasping for breath. He struggled to get free but Maxwell was bigger and stronger and very angry.

From somewhere above them, Tommy's voice came: 'Get up now, Mr Maxwell or I'll blow your brains oot. I'm no' kidding.'

Hector felt the pressure on his throat lessen then stop. Slowly, Maxwell stood up and backed away. Hector blinked and saw Tommy pointing his service revolver at the American. He took a deep, shuddering breath then laboriously got to his feet, pain shooting through his back and his neck. Suddenly, he felt his age. The three men stood eyeing each other, Maxwell breathing deeply, Hector wheezing and gasping for breath. Tommy pointed the gun shakily at the American.

'You'd better give me that, Tommy,' Hector said at length and took his old, familiar weapon, keeping it trained on Maxwell's chest. He used his right thumb to pull back the hammer, hoping that he would not have cause to squeeze the trigger. The shot would sound the death-knell of his career on the bench, and that would be the least of his problems.

A twisted smile spread across the American's face. 'Like I said, you're all hat, no cattle. Your gun's not loaded. I can see the bullet chambers are empty. And judging by his black eye, this kid should leave fighting to the big boys.'

Stunned, Hector was about to lower the revolver when Tommy spoke up: 'There's one bullet in it and it's ready to fire. I wis rushed when I took the gun and there wis just the one bullet in the drawer so I put it in. I didnae have time to search for mair.'

Maxwell stared at him, trying to read him.

Hector kept his revolver and bullets separately. He knew there had been no bullet in the drawer containing the gun; Tommy had to be bluffing. Thinking quickly, he said, 'I hear you like to gamble, Mr Maxwell. During the War I heard that some Russian officers would prove their bravery by loading a gun with a single bullet then spinning the chamber before putting the gun to their head and pulling the trigger. It was known as "Russian roulette". Do you want to play the St Andrews version?' He took aim at the centre of Maxwell's chest, ready to use the revolver as a club if the American attacked again. When no reply came, he continued, 'That's very sensible. When you've done as I tell you you'll leave St Andrews a free man, and you can afford to lose however much money this is going to cost you. Now sit down on that sofa and I'll explain where we stand.'

Tense and wary, Maxwell sat on the sofa. 'Talk,' he said.

It was time for Hector to show his hand. He remembered poker games played at university for pennies. He had been quite adept at keeping a straight face then. Still standing and pointing the gun, he began, 'It will be easy to prove that you have bought the debts run up by the town council, and a lot of town councillors and others, through disastrous investments in America. We can prove your relationship with Mr Feinstein and with the Enright Bank. We can also prove that pressure has been exerted on these debtors to vote for the sale of the golf courses to you; their debts would be forgiven if they voted for your scheme. I have the letter in mirror writing sent by you or on your instructions to the late Mr Corbett. Mr Torkington will give evidence about the letter he received, and the evidence of Mr Haversham will be the final nail in your coffin. The inference that you have been corruptly influencing these men will be irresistible, and you will certainly go to jail.' He paused, aware that he was being scrutinised for any sign that he was bluffing, which he was. Haversham would make a hopeless witness, a gift for any competent cross-examiner. He hoped Maxwell would not realize that. Conviction would be far from certain. Moreover, Hector remembered that the maximum penalties under the statute were surprisingly lenient.

'As I said, I will arrange for you to be arrested on charges of corruption if you are not out of the country on Monday morning.' That was another bluff; he could not imagine Inspector McTaggart arresting this prominent American on the basis of what he could place in front of him. 'Now, please will you sit at that desk, take a piece of hotel writing paper and give a written discharge of the debts owed by this town and its citizens.'

Maxwell sat quite still, his anger under control, his expression hard to read. 'If I do all that, I won't hear any more about this business?'

'I won't do anything, and if anyone else tried, you'd be long gone.'

'I guess that'll have to do.' He got up and sat at the desk. A sheet of Grand Hotel writing paper in front of him, he took one of the hotel pens, wrinkled his nose at it and dipped it in the inkwell.

'Please write the following.' At dictation pace Hector continued, ' "I, Brian Maxwell do freely promise that as at 9.00 pm tonight, British Summer Time, all debts owed to me by the town council of the Royal Burgh of St Andrews, and all debts owed to me by any person currently living in St Andrews or within four miles of the St Andrews main post office will be discharged and unenforceable." Then sign it and date it.'

Maxwell finished writing and handed the paper to Hector, who checked it before putting it in his pocket. Tommy frowned; Maxwell had given in too easily for comfort.

Hector continued, 'I believe you are due to meet a group, mostly town councillors, in a private room at seven-thirty. I shall meet them and explain the situation. I shall also cancel the dinner you have booked for them and arrange for the journalists due to arrive later to be told that you have no comment to make.'

Maxwell, still at the desk, aimed a sullen glare at him.

Hector was not finished. 'I understand that you have been trained as a lawyer. You may be under the illusion that the discharge you have just granted is not binding on you. It does not have what English, and I believe American, lawyers call consideration, namely some benefit going in both directions as part of the contract. But remember we are in Scotland. Scots law regards unilateral obligations as binding and they can be proved by the writ or oath of the granter. This promised discharge I have in my pocket is written by you and will be valid, I can assure you.' This time he was not bluffing.

The effect of these words was dramatic. Maxwell got to his feet, seized a crystal whisky decanter from the sideboard next to him and drew back his arm to throw it. 'Get the hell outa here, punk,' he yelled.

'Goodbye, Mr Maxwell,' Hector said as he followed Tommy out into the hallway. As he closed the door behind him there was a crash of shattered glass.

They made their way along the corridor and down the stairs, Hector still holding the revolver.

'Be careful with that gun, sir,' Tommy said once they had reached the floor below. 'There's a bullet ready to fire.'

Hector stopped in his tracks and put the revolver in safe mode. 'But that was nonsense about the single bullet in the drawer. I thought you were kidding.'

Tommy made sure they were not being followed. 'I remembered you had that gun, sir, and when I told Mrs Drummond I wis going to help you I asked if I could borrow it. I'd heard some bad things about Mr Maxwell in the caddie shed. She didnae like the idea at all, but in the end she got the gun for me. I asked about bullets and she wis really unhappy, but I managed tae wheedle one bullet out of her and she helped me to put it where it would fire. I promised her I wouldnae fire unless I had to. I hope ye dinnae mind, sir.'

'Of course not, but where did you hide it?'

'Doon the back of my troosers. Mrs Drummond showed me how to put the safety catch on in case I shot my own bum.'

Hector smiled, glad he had insisted in showing Lavender how the gun worked in case she ever faced an emergency and he was not about. 'Well could you put it back there now? I don't want to have it on me when I meet these councillors.' He rotated the barrel so that the bullet was no longer in the firing chamber then handed it over.

After checking the safety catch, Tommy reached round and shoved the revolver down the back of his trousers. They continued down the stairs.

When they arrived at the ground floor, O.B. pounced on them, asking how they had got on. Promising to tell him, Hector asked if he would set up whiskies for them somewhere they would not be overheard. Tommy went with O.B. while Hector waited for Mary to be free at reception then relayed his instructions regarding the councillors, the dinner and the journalists.

'Do you still want me to tell Mr Maxwell that the phones are busy, my lord?' she asked.

'I don't think so. I don't want anything to stop him from leaving town,' he replied. After thanking her again he went to join the others.

Beginning to relax, and savouring a fine malt and a cigarette, Hector told O.B. what had happened.

'That's good, Hector,' O.B. said, 'Remind me never to play poker with you. But what if it was Maxwell who killed Macmillan? He may have felt he had reason to do so. I know he wasn't at the play so couldn't have killed Corbett. But have you not encouraged a prime suspect for Macmillan's murder to leave town?'

Hector grimaced. Lavender would think the same, he was sure of it. Had he put a duty he felt to St Andrews before the interests of Jake? 'I don't know who killed either victim, but I have a strong feeling it was the same man. I don't think Maxwell's absence will harm Jake's chances. It might look as if he's fled because he killed Macmillan and felt the net closing in.'

O.B. looked at him and shrugged. 'I guess you know what you're doing.'

Changing the subject, Hector asked how Jones was feeling ahead of the thirty-six hole final against England's Roger Wethered the following day.

'A lot better than he felt earlier today. He always reckons that over one round the better player is vulnerable. He's lost a few eighteen-hole matches to players he'd normally expect to beat. Over two rounds he can wear down his opponent with sustained good golf. He respects Roger, no doubt about it, but he knows he has the beating of him, particularly over thirty-six holes. Roger's a funny guy,' O.B. continued, 'he's a very good golfer but he doesn't take it seriously. You know that, here at St Andrews in 1921, he tied Jock Hutchison for the Open Championship? Well, Bob and some others had to persuade him to compete in the play-off the next day rather than go and play in some small-time cricket match he'd agreed to play in. I guess you'd say he's a true Corinthian, but Bob couldn't understand it. Roger lost the play-off and Jock became Champion, but I reckon he was beaten before a shot had been hit.'

'And tomorrow Bob will really want to win, while Roger will just go out, play as well as he can and see what happens,' Hector said.

'That's the fascinating thing about Bob,' O.B. said, 'he has this intense desire to win, but he must win fairly. He was pretty hurt that some people thought he deliberately aimed at the crowd at the Road Hole against Tolley. He sure tried to get the people to move back.'

'I know, I saw him,' Hector said, 'and Tommy got his black eye standing up for Bob in the caddie shed. If you want to know who was saying he aimed for the crowd, look for a caddie with two black eyes.'

O.B. patted Tommy's knee. 'Thank you, Tommy. I'll tell Bob some day. I know he'll be mighty grateful.'

Hector asked, 'I've often wondered why Bob doesn't become a professional. There's quite a bit of money in the game now and he'd do very well.'

O.B. took a hefty swallow of whisky, choosing his words carefully. 'He genuinely regards it as an absorbing recreation, not a career. Of course he is particularly good at it and he takes it very seriously indeed, but he has a clear intention of working as a lawyer. His father, whom you will remember, is not a rich man but he has been able, indeed happy, to pay for Bob's travel and hotels. I've been around them a lot and I've never been aware of either of them contemplating Bob becoming a professional.

'Because he cares so much about his performance in competitions, they take an awful lot out of him. Even when he was only twenty-three he told me that if he could win a championship in each of the next three years he'd be willing to call it quits. "I can't keep fooling around with this thing much longer" were his words. I'll always remember them. Of course he's twenty-eight now and hasn't called it quits, but it's his place in the record books that motivates him. He hasn't won this great championship yet, and he wants it with all his soul. If he wins tomorrow, he'll want to win your Open at Hoylake more than ever. Then it's our Open at Interlachen and finally our Amateur at Merion. Imagine if he could win them all in one year! He could never do that as a professional. As I say, it's getting his name on the great trophies that drives him, and when he's done he'll go contentedly and practise law.'

'He'll be a very good lawyer too, very principled,' Hector said. He looked at his watch. 'It's time I got ready to meet these councillors. Do you want to come, Tommy?'

'Yes sir.' He swallowed the last of his whisky and got up.

Hector said, 'I'll see you tomorrow O.B. Wish Bob luck from me.'

'And me,' Tommy added.

*   *   *

The private room Maxwell had reserved was spacious. On one side was a table laden with an assortment of drinks and glasses. On the other was a longer table covered in a white cloth. Waiters were removing the last items of cutlery from a setting for dinner. Hector took a seat behind the longer table

and gestured for Tommy to sit beside him. 'I don't expect there
will be anything to worry about, but keep alert in case there
is,' he told him.

Maxwell's guests arrived in dribs and drabs, registering surprise when they saw Hector and Tommy. Hector invited them to
take a drink and sit down if they wanted. By seven-thirty fourteen men dressed for dinner had joined them. Most had taken
drinks and lit cigarettes. All looked wary. Hector knew them
all, a dozen councillors plus Freddie Torkington and Clive Matthews, who were on the Joint Green Committee. John Arnott,
the provost, whom Hector regarded as being completely feck-
less, stood apart from the rest looking scared. Both Torkington
and Jim Liddell aimed concerned glances at Hector, the deep-
ening wrinkles on Liddell's face making him more chimp-like
than ever.

Hector rapped the table to gain attention. There was imme-
diate silence. 'Mr Maxwell will not be joining us,' he said. 'There
have been a number of developments since the vote in the town
council this morning. First, our Member of Parliament, Mr Haversham, has made the following statement to the press. It will
be in tomorrow's papers.' He read out Haversham's statement
to gasps of astonishment. 'As an Act of Parliament would be
required to sanction the sale of the golf courses, that kills Mr
Maxwell's proposal stone dead.' He paused to let that sink in.
'But there is more. I am aware that the town and a number of
you personally have lost considerable sums of money through
unsuccessful investments in American stocks. I am also aware
that Mr Maxwell has bought all these debts. I can reassure
you that he has this evening discharged them. He has written
the following in his own hand and signed it. I am sure that
it will be binding on him under Scots law.' He then read out
the discharge. Looking round, he saw expressions of disbelief

and happiness. Freddie Torkington's Adam's apple wobbled as his face lit up. Some continued to frown. Hector continued, 'The dinner that you have come for has been cancelled. You will understand why. That is all I have to say, except that I am delighted that a serious threat to our town has been lifted.'

A stunned silence was broken by Jim Liddell, who asked what role Hector had played in these events.

'I'm not prepared to answer questions,' Hector said. 'So far as I am aware, the press will not know about the discharge, although news of it will doubtless come out at some time.'

'Why are you not prepared to answer questions?' Liddell insisted. 'Has it anything to do with your boy being charged with murder?'

Hector ignored him.

The meeting was over and the men finished or put down their drinks then left in small groups, Hector watching them closely. Those not noted as being clients of Macmillan's, Provost Arnott included, continued to appear puzzled and concerned.

'You havnae pleased them all sir,' Tommy commented after the last one had left.

'I wonder why,' Hector replied, springing to his feet. 'You stay here.' He ran out, hoping to find someone he could question.

He caught up with Dan Saunderson at the main door. 'Dan, may I have a word?' he panted.

'Yes,' Saunderson responded without enthusiasm. He was a big man from the North of England. His face was red and weather-beaten, his hands red and chaffed. For some years his fish shop in Market Street had sold the freshest catch in town. Recently elected to the town council, he was known for his robust common sense if not his sophistication. He called a spade a shovel. Hector had played against him in the annual match between the town and the R and A. He had liked him then, but remembered his consumption of whisky had been more impressive than his golf.

'I couldn't help noticing that the news of the discharge didn't seem to please you much. May I ask why not?'

The big man's shoulders twitched and he screwed up his face. 'I've nowt to say to thee,' he said, his voice quieter than normal.

'Have you received a threatening letter, urging you to vote for the sale of the courses?' Hector insisted.

'Like I said, I've nowt to say,' Saunderson spat out. He opened the door and left the hotel before Hector could try again.

Hector returned to the private room and poured small whiskies for himself and Tommy. He lit a cigarette without thinking then offered one to Tommy, who took it. 'Saunderson didn't want to talk,' he said.

'We havnae got to the bottom of this business yet, sir. There's been something right fishy going on.' He sniggered.

Hector grinned. 'You're a hopeless valet and a worse music hall comedian, but you're a fine bodyguard and a good detective. Come on, once you've finished your dram and your fag I'll give you a lift home and we can see how your sister is.'

They entered the house in Bridge Street quietly in case Jeannie was sleeping but they found her sitting up in bed. Tommy's mother was much more cheerful than she had been earlier.

'Thae poultices have done her good,' she reported. 'There's a wee bit of burning to her chest, but naething serious. Dr Moncur called this afternoon and wis right pleased wi' her.' She turned to Hector. 'Thank you sir, for getting her. She's saved Jeannie's life, I do believe.'

Hector did not stay long. Tommy told him that he planned to watch the final the next day and he said he hoped to do so too. As he went to the door, Tommy called him back.

'You forgot this, sir,' he said, pulling the revolver from the waistband of his trousers.

'Thomas Addison, whit are you doing wi' that?' his mother exclaimed.

'He probably saved my life,' Hector said, leaving any fuller explanation to Tommy.

Driving home, his satisfaction with the day's events was tempered by the fact that he was no nearer to working out who had murdered Macmillan and Corbett. With Jake still in custody, Lavender would not be happy.

19

Lavender was impatient for news. She had already eaten and was pacing up and down, looking out for Hector's car in the driveway. As soon as he got in she pulled him into the sitting room. He told her briefly what he had done and thanked her for giving Tommy the revolver.

'He didn't fire it, I hope?' she asked.

'He didn't need to, thankfully, but it saved me from a beating, or worse,' he added, the pain in his throat reminding him of Maxwell's crushing grip. If Tommy had not come to his aid, would he have been throttled?

She listened, appalled and concerned, as Hector described Maxwell's violent reaction and Tommy's intervention. Without further ado she ordered him upstairs to their bedroom, where she inspected his neck and his back, which was hurting badly.

'There's a huge bruise coming up,' she told him. 'I'm going to telephone Dr Doris. You may have broken a rib.'

'What about Henry McNaughton?'

'She's his assistant and he's probably three sheets to the wind by this time on a Friday night. I'm going to get Doris.'

His protests in vain, he followed her back down to the sitting room. 'Best not say I've been scrapping,' he warned her. Once she had finished on the telephone they resumed their discussion. He stressed that Macmillan's change of sides could well have brought about his murder. She quickly grasped that the list of potential suspects had lengthened. 'Do you believe that Haversham knew nothing about the letters?' she asked.

'I think I do,' he replied. 'I can understand him not wanting to know too much about Maxwell's methods.'

'Maxwell has got these prominent citizens to vote for him, and it seems that it was not always because of financial pressure. Did they support him because they thought the scheme was a good one?'

'I doubt it.'

'So he had other methods of applying pressure?'

'Probably.'

'Are we talking about thugs and protection rackets? If so, are we safe here? Look at you, and Macmillan and Corbett have been bumped off.' Her voice caught as she thought of Marie and Charlotte, upstairs in bed.

He held her hand. 'I know, but a New York thug would stick out like a sore thumb in St Andrews. Maybe there was something more subtle, some sort of threat to Saunderson's business or family short of violence.'

'Did he have someone local who was helping him?' she asked.

'And if so, who is it? It could be anyone,' he said, answering his own question.

'But if Maxwell was behind these murders, don't we want the police to question him? You've driven him away and he's leaving Jake to face the music.'

'He wouldn't admit anything, darling, here or anywhere else. If he was behind the murders and he leaves town in disarray, that gives us our best chance of finding the truth. And it makes him look guilty,' he added.

Before Lavender could respond the doorbell rang. They heard the doctor's loud voice asking Mrs Alves where the sheriff was.

'I'll do the talking,' Hector whispered as the door opened.

'What have you been up to?' Doris Moncur asked, briskly cheerful. She wore slightly grubby, shapeless trousers and a jersey under which her ample breasts moved freely.

'An accident in the Club. There was a fellow who'd had a bit much to drink. He tripped and fell on top of me. I was leaning back in a chair and it sort of collapsed under me. He fell with his arm across my throat. Damned silly fool.' He smiled ruefully.

Doris looked at his throat and raised an eyebrow. 'Well best have a look at you. Can you climb the stairs?'

In his bedroom, Doris examined him carefully. There was something about the way her hands touched him that gave him confidence that she knew what she was doing, even when it hurt.

'Your throat's bruised and will get better without any treatment. You may well have cracked one or two ribs. There's no displacement that I can detect, but we should be careful and I'm going to apply a firm bandage to your chest.' Hector nodded meekly. 'It's lucky Lavender telephoned when she did. I was about to run a bath,' she commented as she wound a length of crepe round his chest and over one shoulder. 'Keep the bandage on for a couple of weeks and let me know if the pain gets worse,' she instructed, making to leave the room. 'And no more horseplay,' she added with a grin.

'I don't think she believed my story,' Hector said to Lavender, as he relaxed with a whisky and a cigarette, 'but she's jolly thorough. She even had a good look at my eyes. I told her they'd never been the same since the mustard gas.'

'They're even more bloodshot than usual, and I can see

finger marks round your neck. She will realize that someone has tried to strangle you.'

'That's too bad. Have you heard any more about Jake?'

'Mr Hotchkiss telephoned. He'd seen Jake this morning. He said he was being very brave ...' her voice caught, 'but he's so worried and unhappy. I can't bear it, Hector. We have to get him out. We have to.' She dissolved into tears. Hector sat beside her on the sofa, cuddling her and wishing he was nearer to finding the real murderer.

'You'll need to eat,' she sniffed. 'Mrs Alves has a plate of cold meat ready for you. Let's go through to the dining room and we can talk there.'

'How's Bert?' he asked.

'Fine. He's been a great help to Mrs Alves and he read the girls a story before bed. He's a nice boy.'

'Before I eat I'll tell him the good news.' They went to the kitchen where they found Bert ironing one of Hector's shirts while Mrs Alves put the finishing touches to the plate of cold meat. Hector sat at the kitchen table and asked if he might speak to Bert alone. The valet looked anxiously at Hector but as he listened, apprehension turned to delight. When he heard that it was unlikely he would need to give evidence, his face lit up with relief. Hector continued, 'So you'll stay here until Monday morning, when you and I will go to the bank. I'll withdraw the money and give it to you. Then you can take the train to Glasgow. If you continue to be helpful, I'll even pay you for what you've done here.' He grinned.

'There's no need ...' Bert began.

'Nonsense. You have no idea how much help you have been.' He got up and, leaving the valet re-reading his glowing reference, went to the dining room, satisfied that he had accomplished something for the boy.

Deciding to reward himself with a good wine, he went to the pantry where he opened a bottle of Chateau Batailley from the wonderful 1920 vintage. As Lavender watched impatiently, he poured some to let the wine breathe for at least a little time. She brusquely declined a glass. He had barely started to eat when the telephone rang. Mrs Alves came in.

'Excuse me, sir, but are you able to speak to a Mr MacGregor Mitchell? I told him you were having supper,' she added pointedly.

Hector got up quickly, wincing as he did so. MacGregor Mitchell was a second cousin and the unofficial leader of the Scottish criminal bar. In the hall, he grabbed the receiver. 'Gregor, how good of you to call.'

'Hector, it's good to hear your voice. My clerk told me about your difficulty and I've spoken with Mr Hotchkiss. Of course I'll help in any way I can.' His voice was clipped and precise, coloured by a slight Perth accent.

'If it comes to a trial, would you …?'

'Of course. I have told my clerk to keep my diary free around the end of August, when the trial's likely to take place. We can think about junior counsel nearer the time.'

'Thank you, Gregor. We both appreciate that. We do believe Jake is innocent,' he added.

'He is presumed to be innocent, as you well know. He may in fact be innocent, but it is evidence that counts in court and it is from evidence alone that facts can be inferred. From what Hotchkiss tells me there is enough evidence to take Jake's case to a jury. There can be little doubt that the jurors would be entitled to find him guilty of both murders. I believe you have to be prepared for that. I'm not being defeatist, Hector, simply realistic. The police seldom change their minds about a murder after they have charged someone. We have to be prepared for the long haul.'

'That will be very difficult for Lavender.' Unwelcome images flashed through Hector's mind: lines of men in flat caps queuing to get a seat in the public gallery; trumpets announcing a sitting of the High Court; a stern judge on the bench, the black cap available nearby; in the middle of it all, Jake, whey-faced and terrified, his summer lost, trying not to look guilty as he sat in the dock.

'Don't despair. I have confidence in our juries' ability to get it right most of the time. I hope he'll be out and able to caddie for you in the Autumn Meeting.'

Free or not, Hector could not imagine Jake wanting to caddie for him, and anyway that job was Tommy's. 'It's a devil of a hard game when you're involved personally,' he said.

'And it is a game, a desperate and sometimes deadly one; it involves a contest of skill and knowledge and wit with partisan spectators on either side willing their team on to victory. Talking of which,' he added, his tone lighter, 'I heard on the wireless that Roger Wethered is in the final of the Amateur against Bobby Jones. How do you think he'll get on?'

'I expect Bob Jones will win. Actually we've become quite friendly with him and we hope he does.'

'Wethered's a good chap and a fine cricketer. A real Corinthian. I hope it's a good, sporting game.' Hector knew that Mitchell had been an excellent cricketer in his day, with a lethal bowling arm. Now he bowled out crown witnesses, not batsmen.

'Golf is lucky to have men like these at its forefront,' Hector said. Thanking him again, he ended the call. As he returned to the dining room he wondered what he should say to Lavender. He knew there was more evidence against Jake than for him.

Having reassured her that Mitchell would keep himself free for the trial, Hector was spared further interrogation by another ring at the doorbell. This time it was PC Gemmell, again out of uniform. Hector told Mrs Alves to show him into the dining room. When he came in there was an urgency and excitement about his movements. Hector told him to sit down and poured him a glass of wine.

'Has your son had military training at his school, sir?' Gemmell asked before tasting his drink.

'Yes. They wear uniforms and march up and down the quad,' Hector replied, wondering where this might lead.

'Do they learn combat skills?'

'Sometimes they crawl about in the bushes, learning camouflage. Jake enjoyed that. He wasn't so keen on polishing his boots till he could see his face in them. Why?'

'Did they learn how to use a knife or bayonet in combat?'

'No. I don't think so. I hope not. Do you know anything about that, darling?' He turned to Lavender, who was equally puzzled and shook her head.

Gemmell smiled. 'Good. The pathologist who did the post mortems said that both victims were killed in a particular way: the killer stuck the knife into the left side of the neck hard then pulled it across. He believes the two men were killed by the same man, probably someone with combat training, who would have known to keep himself out of the way of the blood spurting from the wound. Inspector McTaggart thinks your son must have learned this as part of his military training at school, but that doesn't seem likely. Also, sir, the bruises found on Mr Macmillan are consistent with your son's account.' He paused, watching Hector and Lavender assess the implications of what he had said.

'Even if Jake does go to trial, MacGregor Mitchell will have something substantial to go on. That must give rise to a reasonable doubt,' Hector said softly. 'Is there any fingerprint evidence?' he asked.

'Both murder weapons were wiped clean. Either that or the murderer wore gloves. It points to a very clear-thinking killer, sir, not a panicky boy.'

'Can McTaggart not see that?'

'Well not yet, sir. I have had a word with the inspector about Mr Torkington, and he says he'll question him himself. I think he may be our man, sir. I really do. He told me he fought in the Boer War and that the Boers were fierce fighters. He would know how to cut a man's throat, he was at the after-play party and he stayed behind after his friends had left the putting green in the *haar*. He says that when he was emptying his bladder,' he glanced at Lavender, 'he heard someone riding a bicycle, just as your son says he did, only it could have been Mr Macmillan's son, who says he took the same route away from the scene.'

Hector nodded. 'Freddie Torkington made no secret of his dislike of Macmillan, even when the man was dead. He says he confronted Macmillan over the anonymous letter he received and he denied having anything to do with it but I don't think Freddie believed him.'

Gemmell produced a sheet of paper with a list of names then continued, full of enthusiasm: 'I've made a list of the councillors who voted for Maxwell's scheme this morning, sir, and only James Liddell was at what they call the Pams' dinner on Sunday and the after-play party on Tuesday. I've questioned some of the others who were at the dinner and they are sure he left the putting green with them and went straight to the New Club. He can't have killed Mr Macmillan. Dennis Bowers was at the dinner but not at the play. Provost Arnott was at the play, with his wife, but left before the party began. The same applies to Daniel Saunderson and his wife. Raymond Macintosh was at the play and stayed for the party but I remember speaking to him after Mr Corbett's murder and he was, frankly, very drunk, sir. I can't see him thinking and acting quickly, as the murderer must have done. And he wasn't at the Pam's dinner. So I keep coming back to Mr Torkington, sir.' He looked from Hector to Lavender.

Hector said, 'Well, I have some news for you. I managed to persuade Mr Haversham to go against Maxwell's scheme. Don't ask me how. But without support in parliament, the so-called Andrean Project is finished.'

'W-well done, sir!' Gemmell stammered as he took a sip of claret. He was consumed with curiosity but understood that it would be better if he didn't know exactly what the sheriff had done.

'And I've persuaded Maxwell to discharge the debts owed to him by the town and its citizens. Again, you don't want to know the details of how I did it.' He gave him a warning look.

Gemmell nodded, his face lit up by a conspiratorial grin.

'Will that include Jane Corbett?' Lavender asked.

Hector smiled. 'Yes. Anyone living within four miles of the St Andrews post office is covered. Jane will be all right.' He paused then added, 'But Haversham lives outwith the four mile area. I'll leave these two scoundrels to work things out for themselves.'

Seeing Gemmell looking puzzled, Hector changed the subject. 'I also learned something very interesting: Macmillan effectively changed sides. He had been advising Maxwell about the governance of the golf courses but drew the line at suing his long-term clients who had lost money through taking his financial advice. He stopped acting for Maxwell and Maxwell didn't like that. It was last Friday that Alan Corbett received an anonymous letter telling him to vote for Maxwell's scheme. I suspect that Freddie Torkington may have got his letter at the same time. He challenged Macmillan about it, as I said, and Macmillan denied all knowledge. Today I learned that last Saturday, Macmillan visited Maxwell at the Grand Hotel and left looking angry. I suspect that Macmillan confronted Maxwell over the letters at that meeting. Who knows, he may have threatened to expose his methods. The people behind the scheme had a motive for silencing him. I didn't care for him, but he was like a terrier; he seldom let a quarrel drop.'

'So Mr Torkington didn't have a motive after all?' Gemmell asked hesitantly.

Hector said, 'In fact, no. But Freddie didn't believe Macmillan's denial of having anything to do with the letter he got. If Freddie did slit his throat, the poor old chump did it because he'd misread the situation.'

'And Jake's paying for it now,' Lavender said. 'I hope we won't regret you telling Maxwell to leave town.'

Gemmell looked sharply at Hector, who shrugged. 'I felt it was best to get him right out of the way. Running would be the sort of thing a guilty man would do. But there's more. When I took over a function at the Grand which Maxwell had organized for this evening and told the councillors who had voted for the scheme about the discharge of their debts, half of them continued to look worried, or at least puzzled, and I happen to know these men were not among those who owed money to Maxwell.' He paused. 'Maxwell must have had some other hold over them, probably not a financial one. A solicitor gets to know all sorts of secrets, but if Macmillan was against blackmailing or bribing councillors, it was not he who gave Maxwell whatever leverage he had over these men. Maxwell must have had an accomplice in the town, someone ruthless enough to threaten councillors, and perhaps, kill Macmillan and then Corbett.'

'Who might that be, sir?'

'I don't know.'

Lavender asked, 'Have you looked at Sorley Macmillan? I could believe that he hated his father, who beat him severely, most recently after he'd been expelled from school. He might have lurked around after his father caught him and Jake, then gone back and killed him as Jake was cycling home. He was at the party, remember?'

Hector said, 'After the play was over he was mooning around a pretty St Leonard's girl, hardly what you'd expect if he was planning a daring, opportunist murder.'

Gemmell said, 'And I don't expect he'll have had any more combat training than your son, ma'am.'

In the silence that followed, Hector finished his meal and Gemmell his glass of wine.

'We've plenty to think about,' Hector said. 'What are you doing tomorrow?'

'Sergeant McNeill and I will be going round with the final. As Mr Jones is playing, there's bound to be a big crowd.'

'I will be there, too,' Hector said, ignoring Lavender's scowl. 'It's amazing how many good thoughts come to you when you're watching sport.' She raised her eyes to the ceiling.

There was little more to be said. They both thanked Gemmell profusely and saw him on his way.

'I really feel that we've emptied all the pieces of the jigsaw onto the table and it's a question of putting them together in the right way,' Hector said as he poured himself more wine and lit a cigarette.

Lavender looked at him coldly. 'I hope you don't mind, but I'll go to bed,' she said, her voice flat.

Hector thought she would be better left alone. He sat smoking and savouring his fine claret. 'What I need is clarity of thought,' he said to himself then laughed quietly at his awful pun.

20

Breakfast the next morning was eaten in silence, the girls realizing that neither Mama nor Papa was in a mood for talking. Hector had a sore head and no appetite for the two boiled eggs awaiting his attention; the Chateau Batailley had failed to clarify his thoughts and the adage that good wine did not give you a hangover had not worked this time. 'You stink of drink' had been the only words Lavender had addressed to him. It was both a surprise and a relief when the telephone rang and Mrs Alves announced that PC Gemmell wanted to speak with the sheriff.

'I can't speak for long, sir,' Gemmell said, his voice low. 'Mr Maxwell's been found dead. In the Cathedral grounds, next to Young Tom Morris' grave. The pathologist's been over from Dundee and it seems he was hit over the head with a champagne bottle then his throat was cut with the neck of the bottle. Probably about ten or eleven o'clock last night. He was found by someone walking their dog about five this morning. There was broken glass and evidence of champagne next to the body but the killer took the neck of the bottle away with him. The pathologist says the glass was thrust into the left side of the neck then pulled across, just like the other murders, sir, so it's probably the same man.'

Hector was staggered. 'Good Lord. Unbelievable. What's going to happen?'

'All I know is I'll be the only policeman on duty for the start of the final. Inspector McTaggart and Sergeant McNeill will be following up on the murder. Inspector McTaggart said he would visit Mr Torkington this morning and bring him in for questioning.'

'Right. Well I'll definitely see you at some stage on the course. This certainly puts a new slant on things.'

'It does that, sir. I must go now. Please don't say I called.'

'Of course not. Thank you very much, Gemmell.'

He put down the receiver and returned to the dining room. When the girls had left the table, he told Lavender the news.

'They should release Jake immediately,' she said.

'It's not as simple as that.'

'Well it should be, and if you'd drunk less last night you'd have been better able to do something about it.'

Feeling that he couldn't win, Hector got ready to go out to watch Jones play in the final.

*   *   *

By the time Hector got to the course a large crowd had gathered round the first tee. There were no parking spaces nearby so he had to drive out along the West Sands road to find somewhere to park the Bullnose. He walked slowly towards the first fairway, worried and deep in thought. As he joined the spectators waiting to see the second shots, Tommy nudged his elbow. He was wearing his usual caddie's clothes, some pomade in his hair the only remnant of his time as a valet.

'Good morning, sir. My, but you look awfu' trachled today.'

Hector started. 'Oh, good morning, Tommy. As a matter of fact, I feel trachled. We've learned a lot about what's happened, but I can't work out who the murderer is; the police are going to question a friend I can't believe is guilty and Jake's still in custody. My wife's very upset. And I drank too much last night,' he added.

Tommy grinned. 'Have you heard about Mr Maxwell, his throat cut beside Young Tom's grave? Rough justice, I say, with him planning to ruin the Old Course.'

'The news has got round fast.'

'It's the talk of the town, sir. But sir, you did good yesterday, real good.'

That made Hector feel better. 'Thank you, Tommy. Look, Bobby Jones is about to plant his second next to the pin.'

Jones' swing looked as smooth as ever but he hit the turf behind the ball, which finished short of the Swilken Burn. The crowd gasped at this most un-Jones like effort and pressed ahead for a view of the tricky chip he had been left with.

Normal play was resumed as Jones clipped the ball sweetly over the burn to within a yard of the hole. The spectators caused congestion at the bridges but Jones waited patiently until the stewards cleared a path for him.

'I'm glad he didn't try to jump the burn like he did in 1927,' an American voice whispered in Hector's ear. It was O.B.

'I remember that. It showed confidence, I suppose, but it could have gone badly wrong,' Hector replied. 'It was an odd risk to take, considering his determination to win that championship.'

They watched in silence as Wethered took two putts and Jones tapped in his short one for the half.

'Thank goodness,' O.B. said. 'That will steady his nerves after that awful second shot. But Hector, you don't look good for someone who's saved this town and the golf course.'

'I can't work out who the murderer is, Lavender's upset with me and I drank too much last night.'

'Wow, that was some hook,' O.B. said as Wethered's drive

at the second rebounded off the railway wall beside the seventeenth fairway. 'Try to relax and enjoy the golf, Hector. Your head will clear and suddenly it may all become obvious.'

It was good advice and Hector concentrated on what promised to be a closely fought match. The final was over two rounds and he knew Jones felt more confident when there was plenty of time for his consistently fine play to wear down an opponent. Helped by an east wind, both players were out in thirty-five and the match was all-square. Conditions for watching were ideal; special trains had been laid on but they had yet to reach St Andrews; the crowd was orderly and formed wide semi-circles round the players. There was little for Gemmell and the stewards to do.

Wethered missed a short putt on the tenth and, into the wind, his long game became ragged. After a topped second at the fourteenth, his ball finished just short of Hell Bunker. Sensing that the match was at a crucial stage Hector, standing on the slope behind the player, became aware that the man beside him was Sidney Roper, Jones' first round opponent.

'Good morning, Mr Roper. I hope you've enjoyed your stay in St Andrews?'

Roper looked at him steadily then spoke in his distinctive English accent. 'You're the gentleman who invited me to stay on after the play?'

'Yes, quite so.'

'Well thank you, I have enjoyed my visit. I didn't expect to get far in the championship but I decided to take a week's holiday and it has been most pleasant.' He paused to watch Wethered play his shot, which reached the green. 'He can't afford to go too many down,' he commented.

'Have you seen the sights? There are some fine historical ruins,' Hector asked as they pressed forward.

'I have. I bought a little book of St Andrews ghost stories. I don't sleep well and I have walked round the streets at night hoping to hear Archbishop Sharp's coach rattling along the west road or perhaps to see the monk falling from St Rule Tower. One night I thought I saw the White Lady of the Haunted Tower gliding along the Cathedral wall, but perhaps it was just a trick of the moonlight.' He shrugged then continued, 'I have had some other strange encounters on my walks, with real people.' He turned and looked at Hector.

'Such as?' he asked, remembering their collision at the West Port after breaking into Macmillan's office.

'Someone bumped into me at the old stone gate into the town a few nights ago. But I didn't recognize him.' He paused again, his lips forming the vestige of a smile, a slight twinkle in his eye. 'Anyway, I didn't want to get involved in other people's business. I did see the late Mr Maxwell a couple of times near the Cathedral and we wished each other a good night. Maybe he had an interest in the White Lady too.'

'What was he doing?'

'Just walking when I saw him. I took it he had the same difficulty sleeping that I have.'

They had reached the green and saw Jones win another hole with a birdie four. Hector wished Roper well for his journey back to Nottingham and walked on, digesting the information he had just received.

Could it have been Freddie Torkington who had met and killed Maxwell in the grounds of the ruined Cathedral? Hector found it hard to see him as a ruthless killer. And what would the hangman do? Would Freddie's tiny chin be enough to stop the rope from sliding over his head? It was funny in a way yet not remotely funny.

Wethered lost the fifteenth and sixteenth and Jones stood

on the seventeenth tee five up, having taken no more than four on any hole. After a hooked drive, Wethered hit a wonderful, long brassie into the wind that finished on the narrow shelf of green. Jones' second, a fraction too far left, ended in the Road Bunker. Hector found a spot immediately behind the bunker, ideally placed to see Jones' recovery. By now the crowd had swelled. The spectators on the other side of the green were tightly packed, those at the front actually on the putting surface. Behind them was a bank leading down to the rough surface of the road where an over-hit or thinned shot from the bunker should finish.

Hector looked past Jones at these spectators and didn't believe what he saw. Among those on the putting surface was Alan Corbett. He seemed to be looking at him with great intensity. Hector blinked and wiped his eyes. Meanwhile Jones had gone into the bunker to play his shot. As he prepared to play, the stewards realized that the press of bodies would stop an over-hit recovery from going onto the road and began to order them back. Remembering the controversy when his ball had been deflected by the crowd at the same hole in the Tolley match, Jones smiled and stepped out of the bunker. Hector scanned the moving faces opposite but Corbett's was no longer there. He was sure of what he had seen and it shook him. His mind far from the golf, he was dimly aware of Jones waiting until there would be nothing to stop a poor shot from finishing on the road then executing a delicate shot, the ball trickling down the slope from the bunker and coming to rest four feet from the hole.

As Jones missed his putt to lose the hole and take his only five of the round, Hector remembered Jane Corbett saying that Alan's brother, Martin, would be coming to help her. Alan must have had a twin. Then he remembered O.B. commenting on

Alan's performance as Banquo's ghost: he had seemed to be looking accusingly past Macbeth at O.B. as Macbeth delivered the line,

'Thou canst not say I did it: never shake thy gory locks at me'.

Had that moment sealed Alan Corbett's fate? Had Macmillan's murderer believed the accusing stare was aimed at him? Hector tried to remember who had been seated near O. B.

As he followed the players up the eighteenth fairway other questions crowded his mind. Who, apart from solicitors, know the secrets people would want to keep hidden? Who had returned from America recently and now had a splendid new car? Who had known a soldier killed in the War who might have used mirror writing? Might one purpose of the mirror writing have been to disguise handwriting that was liable to be recognized? Who had a distinctive shape and often wore trousers? Who disliked Macmillan personally, quite apart from his opposition to the Andrean Project? Who might have gone after him as he followed Sorley and been seen by Alan Corbett near the eighteenth tee of the Old? Who, apart from those with combat training, would know how to slit a throat and be able to do it quickly and efficiently? He remembered Maxwell's eyes following a well-built lady in the Gleneagles lounge. Lastly, he remembered that Young Tom Morris had died of a broken heart.

As these thoughts went through his mind, the players halved the eighteenth so that Jones went into lunch four up. By the time the golfers left the green, Hector knew what he must do.

Gemmell was on the far side of the green, talking with the stewards. Pushing against the crowd, most of whom were going in the opposite direction, Hector took some minutes to reach him. He grasped the policeman's arm. 'This is urgent,' he hissed.

'I know who did it. All three murders, I mean.' Gemmell turned, ignoring the looks of astonishment on the faces of the stewards. 'Can you meet me at Granny Clark's Wynd in ten minutes? We may need Tommy Addison as well. Have you seen him?'

'I'll be there, sir. And no, I haven't seen Addison.'

Hector made his way, with less difficulty, to the caddie shed and heard the noise of a commotion. He pushed the door and saw two caddies rolling about the floor, trading punches. Around them the other caddies were shouting encouragement to one or the other. One of the fighters was Tommy.

'Stop that at once!' Hector shouted in his best officer's voice.

Tommy looked up first, giving his opponent the chance to land a straight right to his mouth.

'Get up! What's this all about?'

The two youths scrambled to their feet, their faces red. Hector noticed that Tommy's opponent had two black eyes.

Tommy said, 'Stuartie, here thinks Mr Jones wanted to play his bunker shot before the crowd moved on the Road Hole so his ball could bounce off them.'

'Is that really worth fighting over?' Hector laid a hand on Stuartie's shoulder. 'You can think what you want, Stuartie, but is that likely behaviour from a man who has lost a United States Open through calling a shot on himself when his ball moved and no one else could have seen it? Bobby Jones always plays very briskly. I think he would have visualised the shot he was going to play and the idea that he might go onto the road simply wasn't in his mind at all. That's just what I think.'

Stuartie looked down. 'Aye, maybe sir.'

'Are you going to shake hands?' Hector asked.

Stuartie's hand was the first to come out. Tommy took it reluctantly.

'Well let's have no more of this then,' Hector said then addressed Tommy. 'Can you come with me now?'

As they walked down the eighteenth fairway towards Granny Clark's Wynd Hector said, 'You know, you should try to win arguments with your brain and your tongue. You'll find it less painful and you'll probably be more successful.'

Tommy used his sleeve to wipe blood from his lip then muttered, 'I like a good fecht every now and again.'

Hector shook his head. 'You might find yourself in another one very soon, but I sincerely hope not.'

* * *

Gemmell was waiting when they reached Granny Clark's Wynd. He and Tommy eyed each other suspiciously. Once more in army officer mode, Hector addressed them both.

'I am as certain as I can be that, surprising as it may seem, the person who murdered Gordon Macmillan, Alan Corbett and Brian Maxwell was Dr Doris Moncur.'

'But she saved our Jeannie,' Tommy blurted out.

'She's an outstanding doctor but I believe she was both Maxwell's lover and his accomplice in the Andrean Project and that last night she killed him, presumably after he had ended their affair. If I am right she is likely to flee or do something desperate before the law catches up with her. If we go to her house now we may be able to stop her. There is no time to lose. Her brother may intervene on her behalf, so I have asked Tommy to help us. The rest of the local police are busy elsewhere, so it may have to be a citizen's arrest, which would be quite legal in the circumstances.' Without waiting for a response he set off across the main road to Cupar and up Windmill Road, Tommy and Gemmell following.

The rose beds on either side of the Moncurs' garden path were poorly kept, in need of pruning, fertilizing and weeding. The paint on the front door was chipped and dirty. Hector kept his finger on the doorbell longer than necessary then looked around anxiously. Willie Moncur opened the door, a worried expression on his face. He did not hide his surprise at seeing his three visitors.

'Is Doris in, Willie?' Hector asked before Willie could speak.

'Er, yes. She's in.'

'We must see her now.'

'What's wrong? Has there been an accident? Is someone ill?'

'I can't say now, but we must see her.' He stepped up into the doorway, making Willie back away.

'What's wrong? Please tell me what's happening.'

'You'll know soon enough,' Hector insisted. 'I'm truly sorry, Willie.' He moved past him into the hallway. Tommy and Gemmell followed. 'Where is she?'

Willie scratched his head in distress. 'She was in a dark mood at breakfast, hardly said a word. She went into her surgery as soon as she'd finished and hasn't come out. Cook tried calling her for lunch but she didn't reply. I tried the door of her surgery but it was locked. What's wrong?'

Hector pointed to a door at the far side of the hall. 'That's the surgery there, isn't it?'

Willie nodded. Hector turned the handle but the door stayed shut. 'Do you have a key?' he asked.

'No. She has the only one. She must have locked it from the inside.'

'We'll have to break the door down,' Hector said.

'Wait a minute, sir,' Tommy said, squatting and peering through the keyhole. 'The key's in the lock. I think I can get it. Can you get me a sheet of newspaper and a bit of wire?' he asked Willie.

Willie hurried away, returning with a copy of *The St Andrews Citizen* and some wire pipe cleaners. Tommy took a sheet of paper and slid it across the wooden floor so that it was under the lock on the other side of the door. Inserting a pipe cleaner into the keyhole, he poked and prodded until the key fell out of the lock, dropping onto the paper. Carefully, he pulled the paper back under the door, the key on it.

'I won't ask who taught you that trick,' Gemmell muttered.

'Well done, Tommy,' Hector said as he turned the key and opened the door.

The doctor was sitting in her chair behind her large desk. Her head lolled back and her mouth was open. Her eyes stared at the ceiling. Beside the contraption with the rubber airbag Hector had observed on his previous visit was an empty bottle of Glenmorangie, a glass containing a light brown liquid and an empty pill bottle. Hector picked it up.

'Luminol, a barbiturate,' he commented. He shook her gently and felt her neck for a pulse. 'I'm sure she's gone, but we'd better fetch Henry McNaughton. Or Dr White.'

Willie slumped into the chair used by patients and let out a wail of anguish. He covered his face with his hands and began to sob. Hector put a hand on his shoulder. Gemmell seized the telephone and asked for Dr McNaughton as a matter of urgency. Tommy picked up three sheets of writing paper lying on the blotter and handed them to Hector. 'This is for you, sir.'

Ignoring Gemmell's look of concern, Hector read out loud:

'For Sheriff Hector Drummond:

'Dear Sheriff Drummond,

'I am addressing this to you as I suspect you may work out

what has happened and be the one who finds me. I also respect your integrity.

'First, please read this to my dearest brother, Willie: Willie, you have suffered terribly through your inability to read and write properly. I know you are no fool. You have been unfairly treated all your life. Had the Andrean Project come to fruition, you would have been the professional for the club we were going to create and I would have made sure you had the loyal support of someone who could read and write, leaving you to do what you are good at. It was better that you should not know what Brian Maxwell and I were doing. I apologise for keeping you in the dark, and I am sorrier than you can imagine to be leaving you in this manner. All I can say is that it is better than the alternative: prison, trial then hanging. Farewell, my dearest brother. May we meet one day in a happier after-life. Your loving sister, Doris.'

Willie shook his head and continued to weep silently.

Hector continued: 'Sheriff Drummond, as you may have guessed, Brian Maxwell and I had an affair that began some time ago but became serious this spring. He wanted to bring St Andrews into the twentieth century, with a better hotel and an improved golf course run by a modern club. He wanted, in his phrase, "to run these dinosaurs into the North Sea". So did I. I can honestly say that for the last two years I have been the best qualified, most up-to-date, hardest working doctor in the town, yet few of Henry McNaughton's patients want to see me. Most will transfer to Dr White's practice when Henry retires. I had always resented the way this town has treated my dear brother and I came to resent the way they treated me, laughing behind my back because they thought I couldn't attract a man.

'I believed Brian Maxwell loved me, but I now see I was a gullible fool, seduced by big ideas, big talk and big money. He used me. He told me he could put financial pressure on various people and the town itself, but he needed more. I am ashamed to say I gave away secrets no doctor should divulge except for a good reason. I can say only that I considered my reason to be good.

'I knew about alcoholism, about children born out of wedlock, about wives who didn't just bump into doors. I knew about venereal disease and about long-forgotten relatives rotting in some hideous lunatic asylum. I used that knowledge, concealing my handwriting by using a mirror. I had done this in correspondence with the real love of my life, who was taken from me at the very end of the War. And it nearly worked. Brian was on the threshold of success when you intervened.

'I had to kill Macmillan and anyway I wanted to; he treated his wife and son disgracefully and brutally. Brian and I needed to keep our affair secret. When he was in St Andrews we met at night in the Cathedral grounds. We would walk round the ruins, dreaming and planning. It was a fine place for us to make love. Last Saturday he told me Macmillan had threatened to expose what we had been doing with the letters. I couldn't let that horrible man spoil my life, prevent our wonderful plans from coming to fruition. I saw Sorley sneak out on Sunday night and I saw Macmillan following him. I decided to go after them and when the *haar* came in and I found Macmillan lying unconscious in that clearing, I seized my opportunity.

'I regret killing Alan Corbett, but during that play when he was supposed to be a ghost he stared at me so accusingly that I was sure he had identified me. That was reinforced by what he said afterwards. I had to act swiftly and decisively and that's what I did.

'I am sorry that your son has had such an ordeal. You may remember that I asked about representation and you told me you would engage the best counsel. I took comfort from that; there would have been too many holes in the prosecution case to convict an innocent man. Had the trial gone against him, please believe me that I would have found some way of confessing and saving him.

'The plan was that Brian and I should marry and live in the United States. That is a young, energetic country where my abilities would be respected. Last night, in the Cathedral grounds, my dreams came crashing down. Brian told me what you had done and that we were finished. I had brought champagne, believing we had a success to celebrate. We were at Young Tom's grave when he told me that he had never loved me. I hit him with the bottle, stunning him. The bottle shattered. There was a long shard of glass at the neck and I used it to cut his miserable throat. My heart had been broken, like Young Tom's.

'I can feel the pills and the whisky doing their job. Please pray for me.

'Doris Moncur.'

'That's clear enough,' Hector said as he folded the sheets of paper and put them in his inside pocket.

'But Sheriff, Inspector McTaggart will want to see that himself,' Gemmell said anxiously.

'It was addressed to me and it is my document,' Hector said. He feared that McTaggart would delay Jake's release for as long as possible.

'I have to protest, sir,' Gemmell insisted. 'This is important evidence and should be held by the police.'

'And you have protested, as your superior would expect, but you have protested in vain. It wasn't the police who got to the bottom of this business. Come on, Tommy.' He patted Willie's shoulder. 'I'm very sorry,' he said then, at the door, turned back to Gemmell. 'Thank you. You are the best sort of police-man and I appreciate the difficulty you're in.'

Out in the street, Hector thanked Tommy for all his help. While the caddie went off to watch the second round of the final, Hector went to his car and drove home. At last he had good news for Lavender.

*   *   *

Lavender was in the sitting room, reading, when Hector burst in. The cool look she gave him changed to one of astonishment then delight as he told her what had happened.

'Doris? I can't believe it, yet it all makes sense,' she said. 'Where does that leave Jake?'

'They'll have to release him. The only question is when. I'm going to telephone Newton, the procurator fiscal. He's a good man and will do his best, but we may have to wait till next week.'

'That's ridiculous.'

'At least the nightmare's nearly over, darling.' He went to the telephone and asked for Newton's number. Mrs Newton told him that her husband had gone to watch the golf.

With some trepidation, Hector explained to Lavender that he would have to go back to the course to find Newton. She nodded. 'Do your best, Hector, but you're right, the nightmare's nearly over.'

Three years earlier, the procurator fiscal service had been set up to provide every part of Scotland with prosecutors who were independent of the police and answerable to the Lord Advocate, who was a member of the government. They prose-cuted in the public interest, not on the instructions of the police. The new service was settling in nicely and in Newton, Cupar had an intelligent, fair-minded man whom Hector respected.

As Jake's prosecution had begun and he had appeared in court, Newton had the authority to order his release, whatever objections McTaggart might have.

There were many more cars parked out on the West Sands road than earlier in the day. Hector made his way across the Jubilee and New courses to where he thought the final might have reached. As he emerged from the gorse bushes beside the sixth fairway, a huge roar erupted from the green. He could see that the orderly crowd that had followed the players in the morning had swelled to something resembling a mob, with people at the back running about, jostling and shoving. The bunkers on the right of the sixth fairway had their sand churned by many footprints.

'At last Wethered's holed a putt! He's only three down. Let's hope he makes a match of it,' a man replied to Hector's question. It was clear that the trains laid on to bring spectators to St Andrews had been full of people hoping for a British victory but desperate to see Bobby Jones and keen to witness a closely-fought encounter. The prospects of finding Newton in this surging, stampeding horde were not good.

Wethered had given the crowd encouragement with his birdie three at the sixth but Jones won the next two holes with pars to go five up and the final was turning into a procession. When Jones drove the tenth green and won the hole with a birdie, the only question seemed to be: how long would the match last?

As Wethered putted close from long range at the eleventh, Hector spotted Newton. He pushed his way through the press of bodies, ignoring the protests of those whose view he spoiled. When he tugged the fiscal's arm, he was met with an embarrassed smile. 'I must speak with you, Mr Newton, it's very urgent,' he hissed.

Good manners, if nothing else, obliged the fiscal to listen as Hector led him away from the crowd, told him what had happened and showed him Doris Moncur's confession.

He read it carefully. 'Well that changes everything. Do you mind if I keep this, Sheriff?' he asked. 'Obviously you would like your son to be released as soon as possible but this is the weekend and there is some red tape to be cut through. I'll do what I can, but I can't promise anything.'

That was the best Hector could expect. He thanked Newton and, from a hillock on the left of the twelfth, saw Wethered fail to get down in two from a position behind the green. The match was over and Jones had won by seven and six.

Whatever disappointment the crowd may have felt at the lack of a close game did not last. They cheered and mobbed the new champion, anxious to touch him, slap him on the back, lift him onto their shoulders as they had after the 1927 Open and thus claim a connection with him. Four policemen from Cupar were at hand to escort Jones back to the Grand Hotel, an officer gripping each arm as they might restrain a criminal. The stewards struggled to clear a path for them. On the eighteenth, a band had assembled but the crush of bodies prevented them from playing a note.

A distance behind Jones, Hector saw an overjoyed O.B., who was doubly delighted to hear Hector's news.

'You must come to the Grand and see Bob before the prize-giving,' he said. 'He and Mary have been worried for you. You know,' he said wistfully, 'I think Bob's name had been written in the books for this championship before a shot was played. Some men call it fate, but at crucial points of the week, Bob always managed to hit the shot he needed to. He knew this was meant to be and that knowledge affected the way he approached these important shots.'

Back in the safety of his hotel, surrounded by friends and some journalists, Jones said, 'I don't think I was ever so happy about any golf event in my life. I shall do my best in the Open at Hoylake, but I shall not worry if I don't win there. This was the big thing for me.' When he heard Hector's news, he shook his hand warmly. 'I'm delighted, Hector. My, this has been a fine day!'

It was time for the presentation. Amplifiers had been placed in the balcony of the Royal and Ancient, overlooking the first tee so that the champion's smooth Georgia drawl might be heard by the masses thronging the first and eighteenth fairways. Jones hurriedly brushed his hair and put on a jacket then went out to the little veranda in front of the clubhouse. Hector and O.B. found a place in front of the caddie shed where they could witness the ceremony. When Jones grasped the handsome trophy he looked as if he could not believe what was happening. Then, emotion in his voice, he addressed the crowd:

'I must say how happy I am to have won this cup. I have never worked harder or suffered more than in trying to get it. It has been said that I enjoyed the Tolley match, but, much as I love Cyril, I would not have been glad to see him in the next round. I have said before that St Andrews has been a little bit too good to me when I was lucky enough to win the Open here, but I want to say now that it has made me feel happier than ever in the past. The more I play the Old Course the more I love it. It is quite different from anything else in the world. There is just one St Andrews, and I always like to get into its atmosphere. I feel in my heart I have been tremendously lucky this week. I say that quite frankly, but nevertheless I am awfully glad I have been lucky, and I am awfully glad I was lucky at St Andrews.'

Bursting with pride and pleasure, O.B. said to Hector, 'What a wonderful week, and I'm so glad things have worked out for you. I'll say goodbye now. There's been a train laid on to take us and some others to London tonight. Tomorrow Bob and Mary head for Paris. It's been great seeing you again. Send our love to Lavender.'

For Hector it had not been a wonderful week. As he trudged along the West Sands road to collect his car he felt sad, sad that the championship was over, sad that four lives had been lost, sad that Jake was still in custody and, above all, sad that the town he loved should have so embittered a good, caring, clever woman like Doris Moncur.

When he got home, the celebrations were muted. 'I just want my boy back,' Lavender told him, her voice choking.

'Papa, Mama, there's a police car in the drive,' Marie shouted.

'It'll be that ass McTaggart looking for Doris' confession,' Hector said.

There was no ring at the doorbell. Jake walked in and flung his arms round both his parents. Tears of joy flowed freely then Hector broke away from the other two.

'What are you doing?' Lavender asked.

Hector replied, 'I think we should have some port after dinner. I'm going to open a bottle and decant it. The 1904 is finished, but the 1912 vintage wasn't too scruffy. What do you think, Jake?'

POSTSCRIPT

After their holiday in Paris, Bob and Mary Jones returned to Britain. The Open Championship was played at Hoylake and Jones won it by two shots from Leo Diegel and Macdonald Smith. Bob and Mary sailed back across the Atlantic to a ticker-tape reception in New York. After only a few days' practice, Jones teed up in the US Open at Interlachen. In sweltering heat, he won that as well. Two months later, at Merion, one of his favourite courses and in front of a gallery of 18,000, he won the US Amateur Championship. He had achieved what was then golf's Grand Slam. With no more worlds to conquer, he retired from competitive play.

As a non-competitor, his amateur status no longer mattered to him and he made some instructional films for Warner Brothers. Big Hollywood stars were happy to appear as his pupils. He also took an interest in club design and worked on this with the Spalding company.

He wanted to build a golf course that ordinary golfers might enjoy while testing the skills of good players. He found some land near Augusta that appealed to him and with the help of financier Clifford Roberts and course architect Dr Alister Mac-Kenzie, he created the Augusta National. When he invited his friends and the best players of the day to a competition on his new course, the Masters was born.

When America entered the Second World War, despite his age and family responsibilities, Jones enlisted. He served with distinction and reached the rank of lieutenant colonel.

When not otherwise engaged, Jones happily practised law. That was his profession.

A few years after the War, Jones began to suffer from a painful condition affecting his bones. It was permanent and progressive, but slow. He continued to work as a lawyer and act as host at the Masters, but latterly he was badly crippled and in pain. He endured this with good-humoured stoicism. When asked how he was, one day near the end, he replied, 'I have my heart, my lungs and my so-called brain. We play the ball as it lies.' He died on 18th December 1971, a few months short of his seventieth birthday.

After 1930, the love affair between Jones and St Andrews continued. In 1936, he arrived in the town with some friends and played a round on the Old. Word of this spread and a crowd of thousands followed him. In October 1958 he was given the freedom of the Royal Burgh. In a moving ceremony Jones said, 'I could take out of my life everything except my experiences at St Andrews and I would still have a rich, full life.' To this day, an exchange scholarship programme between St Andrews University and Emory University in Atlanta flourishes. It is a great honour to be a Bobby Jones scholar.